WHO IS THE EXECUTIONER?

Meet Mack Bolan, combat hero of Korea and Viet Nam and now a one-man army fighting America's most insidious enemy – the Mafia.

In Viet Nam the military ledgers credit Bolan with more than 90 VC 'Kills'. He was an extraordinary soldier – and a man who worked at his job.

Then he returned home one summer to find his father, mother and sister dead. He traced the crime to a Mafia loan-shark's dealing with his father. That was the beginning of a new direction in Mack Bolan's war career.

'It looks like I have been fighting the wrong enemy,' he said. 'Why defend a front line 8,000 miles away when the real enemy is chewing up everything you love back home?'

Also by Don Pendleton

THE EXECUTIONER: MIAMI MASSACRE
THE EXECUTIONER: NIGHTMARE IN NEW YORK

and published by Corgi Books

Don Pendleton

The Executioner:
Assault on Soho

CORGI BOOKS
A DIVISION OF TRANSWORLD PUBLISHERS LTD
A NATIONAL GENERAL COMPANY

THE EXECUTIONER:
ASSAULT ON SOHO

A CORGI BOOK 0 552 09205 3

First publication in Great Britain

PRINTING HISTORY
Corgi edition published 1973

This book is set 10 on 11 pt. Baskerville.

Corgi Books are published by Transworld
Publishers Ltd.,
Cavendish House, 57–59 Uxbridge Road,
Ealing, London W.5.

Made and printed in Great Britain by
Cox and Wyman Ltd., London, Reading and Fakenham

The Executioner:
Assault on Soho

PROLOGUE

MACK BOLAN's one man war against the Mafia began, as do so many larger wars, as an act of rage, frustration, and vengeance. Bolan himself had admitted this in his personal papers, and he makes no attempt to pose as a hapless victim of circumstances.

'I knew what I was doing,' he states. 'I was out to collect a blood debt from the outfit that destroyed my family. That's all there was to it, at first. Then when my hate wore thin, I began to see that there was a lot more at stake than one man's personal revenge. I stopped hating the enemy and began to understand them, and it became all the more important that I stand and fight to the bitter end. Someone has to stand up to these guys and show them that they are not God almighty. They are not trying to *prove* that they are; they *believe* that they are.

'This *Cosa Nostra* is a religion and a sovereign government and a culture all rolled into one. They think the whole world is theirs for whatever they can gouge or terrorize or shake out of it. Everything they touch turns rotten and every place they stake out begins to eat itself. What do you do with a cancer . . . ask it to kindly go away and die quietly? Not *this* cancer.

'Some newspapers have been calling me the twentieth century Don Quixote. That's okay. Maybe what I'm doing is stupid and even wrong and maybe I am just another idiot fighting windmills, but I don't hear any laughing from the enemy camp. I am doing what I have to do and all I know for sure is that when I stop fighting, I'll stop living. I don't want to stop living with all these little gods still carving up the world into personal territories. I intend to go on fighting until my last breath, and I'm going to shake and rattle and bust that kingdom of evil with everything I have.'

In Bolan's case, 'everything I have' was considerable. He

7

had been a different kind of hero before the Mafia cancer reached into his personal life. He was a U.S. Army sergeant serving a second combat tour in Vietnam, a professional soldier with simple tastes and ambitions, a quiet and friendly man as regarded by his comrades, an extraordinary weapon of war as regarded by his government.

Bolan had been a weapons expert, a skilled armorer for every personal weapon in the army's arsenal, and he was a crack marksman with each of these weapons. His combat experiences also revealed steel nerves, a remarkable instinct for guerilla warfare tactics, and a self-sufficiency which made him a natural for the special role thrust upon him in Southeast Asia, one which earned him the unofficial title. *The Executioner.*

Operating as a sniper team sharpshooter, the young sergeant repeatedly penetrated hostile territories and strongholds in missions requiring that he remain for extended periods behind enemy lines to 'seek out and destroy' Viet Cong military and terrorist leaders. His score was phenomenal, with more than eighty verified VIP 'kills' in the official record book.

Bolan's personal courage and resourcefulness won him the admiration of superiors and comrades alike, and his effect upon the enemy was incalculable in terms of psychological warfare benefits. He was far more than a sniper. Executing an important defector or enemy field commander on his own soil could be a ticklish business. To simply locate and identify the target in unfamiliar territory was challenging enough, and a task of no ordinary dimensions. To then make the strike, remain in the target zone long enough to verify the kill, and to then safely withdraw through miles of aroused enemy country – and to perform such missions repeatedly through two full combat tours – required a decidedly special kind of man. Bolan was that special kind. The enemy recognized this – his name had become a VC epithet, and he was one of the few noncommissioned soldiers in history with a price on his head.

His own nation's government recognized his value also; he was one of the most decorated soldiers of the Vietnam conflict. According to those who knew him best, however, the young sergeant-son of an immigrant steelworker had remained a quiet man with simple tastes and ambitions, a kindly man who repeatedly jeopardized his own safety to assist a wounded comrade or a terrified child or a stricken peasant woman. He took no noticeable pride in his grim speciality and in fact refused to discuss details of his missions with anyone other than his military superiors. Of the several men who knew him intimately, none would agree with the war correspondent who characterized Bolan as a 'cold-blooded and remorseless killer with an Army hunting license'.

In Bolan's own assessment, he was simply a professional soldier doing his job.

Towards the end of his second combat tour, Bolan was called home to bury his mother, his father, and a younger sister. This traumatic homecoming brought a dramatic turn to the young soldier's life. The official police findings in the family deaths were listed as double homicide and suicide, with Bolan's father as villain of the piece. Sergeant Bolan could not accept this verdict, and his own investigation turned up evidence that Sam Bolan, the father, had been squeezed beyond human endurance by a loansharking operation of a local Mafia arm. When the young Bolan girl was pressured into working as a prostitute to help retire a usurious loan, and her father learned about it, the elder Bolan had gone berserk and had killed the girl, her mother and himself.

Mack Bolan could find no blame in his heart for his father's insane actions. He blamed the cancer of organized crime and he quickly learned that there was no possibility of getting justice through official channels. And so it was that *The Executioner* decamped from the problems of Vietnam and opened a new front against the larger enemy at home. The rest is history.

Bolan expected no medals in this new war. He understood and accepted the fact that his actions could not be condoned by American society, and he felt no bitterness at becoming the nation's most wanted 'criminal'. He did, sometimes, feel very much alone. Warfare can be a lonely business for a one man army. Like any other man, he missed the warmth of human friendship and detested the feeling of utter isolation. Like any other man, he suffered the tensions of a constant balance between life and death … he knew fear, and anxiety, and pain, and revulsion and desperation … he had all the feelings of any normal man.

But, in his words, Bolan had 'built my own hell. I can live here, and I guess I can die here. Some things you just have to accept. It seems that I have a job to do, and I accept that. But I do not accept death – that is, I do not seek it. A man can't look for a place to die; he has to take his stand on a way to live. When you do that, death comes naturally in its own time and place.'

An executioner's philosophy? Perhaps. But Bolan's philosophy centered mainly about action. Peripherally, he was incorruptible, non-negotiable, ready to die if necessary, but anxious to live. But his task was to kill the Mafia and this fact provided the central core of his life. A soldier wars to win, and Bolan had long ago demonstrated his dedication to that proposition. He was fighting the impossible fight, yes … but he was fighting to win, not to lose, and he sought not his own death but the death of the enemy, all of the enemy, anywhere and everywhere, for as long as this impossible war could last. And it could last only so long as Mack Bolan could remain alive. Kill to live, and live to kill. No job, this, for the squeamish, or the weak or the non dedicated.

'Some things you just have to accept,' said Bolan. And what he had accepted was a kingdom of evil, a domain of violence, a life of unending warfare.

In Bolan's five previous campaigns against the crime combine, we saw him growing into his destiny and taking the war to the enemy with thunder and lightning which, indeed, shook their 'kingdom of evil' to its very foundations. He succeeded in becoming the most feared man in underworld history and the most sought by the police.

Not only the Mafia and the police want Mack Bolan; a $100,000 open contract with generous additional bonuses has drawn professional and amateur gunmen into the largest bounty hunt of modern times–and although the average man in the street thought of Bolan as a sympathetic and heroic figure, every hand stretched out to him in friendship must be viewed with suspicion. Even a genuine offer of aid carried built-in hazard, both to the ally and to Bolan himself. Allies complicate the battle and broaden the responsibility: Bolan had learned that the violent domain was kinder to him when he walked alone.

At the opening of this account, Bolan has again become 'the cat that walked by himself'. Once again in a strange land he nevertheless discovers that 'all places are alike to him'. The Mafia is there. Bolan is there. And, inevitably, violence and terror and death are there.

CHAPTER ONE

RECEPTION AT DOVER

BOLAN did not see the enemy but he could sense their ominous presence out there, in the darkness. He had felt that from the moment he stepped aboard the car ferry at Calais, and it had lasted throughout the brief crossing of the English Channel and the landing at Dover.

Sure, they were waiting for him: the escape from France had been too smooth, too easy, as though someone had been running interference for him. Even the fast shake through British customs had been entirely too easy. Now that he was in England the feeling had accelerated into a big ball of mush in the pit of his stomach and he knew that he had been maneuvered here, manipulated and channeled and directed to just this place and time. And now they were out there, waiting.

He unbuttoned his coat and tested the breakaway on his side leather, then checked the clip of the hot little Beretta automatic, retracted the slide to chamber in a 9mm round beneath the hammer, and snugged the combat-ready weapon back to his side. The retreat was over.

Bolan had purposely hung back to allow the swirl of debarkation to proceed on ahead of him as he watched and evaluated possible avenues of escape. Now he stepped out of the shadows of the ferry station and into a very light foot traffic, walking at a casual clip toward the waiting railway cars. Footsteps immediately moved in behind him, pacing him across the darkness; a double pair, slowing when he slowed, quickening when he quickened. Bolan's trained ears could recognize a dropback set . . . and as he crossed the fifty yards or so of wharf he became aware also of a converging set across his flanks. He was being bracketed on either side and cut off from the rear. Somewhere up ahead he would find the final side of the box, and this would be a place of their careful choosing, a point of no escape, with doubtful survival for the prey caught in the centre of that box.

Bolan took a deep breath and made his move, pivoting suddenly and walking straight toward the left flank. He heard them quietly adjusting, a soft voice in the darkness behind him issuing muffled commands, a sudden scraping of quick feet just ahead making hurried changes to the choreography, running sounds on his new right flank.

It was time to hit, perhaps the only time he would find. But first he had to make positive identification of the enemy. He had never yet slapped leather on a cop; he had no wish whatever to do so now. A dim overhead lamp, muffled and impotent in a high-swirling fog, lay just across his path. He stopped directly beneath it and lit a cigarette, his ears straining for movements about him, and he found encouragement in the knowledge that they still seemed to be somewhat off balance and scurrying toward new positions on the box. He went on quickly then, looking to neither left nor right but with ears quiveringly alert to the sound behind him.

Now! He flipped the lighted cigarette far ahead, the gun hand moved inside the coat and his forward motion was arrested on the ball of his right foot as he went into his pivot, swinging about to the right in a lightning sweep, the Beretta swinging with him at full extension and spitting its sharp argument against entrapment as Bolan sprawled into a prone firing position. For a single heartbeat Bolan had hesitated, staying the trigger finger and sacrificing that all-important moment of surprise in the interests of identification. But a heartbeat was all that was required; his uncanny timing had caught them directly beneath the overhead lamp, and this split-second of visual reference was all Bolan needed to confirm his earlier instinctive identification ... his welcoming committee were *Mafiosi*.

Earlier that day Bolan had refined the tolerances on the new Beretta and reworked the trigger for a four-pound pull, getting consistent two-inch target groupings in rapid fire from twenty-five yards. Tonight he was thankful for that foresight, even though firing at an almost point-blank ten-yard range. The two men under the lamp were dead on their feet with mutilated hearts, pistols hardly clear of the side-leather, and even as they fell Bolan was rolling on. Then he gathered his feet under him, and charged the side of the box. Muzzle flashes pierced the darkness ahead of him as hand-guns were unloaded in panicky reaction and fired blindly at him, the unseen and fast moving target. Even so, Bolan was moving through a suddenly dense atmosphere, and the flash-ing synapses of his computer-quick brain told him that the enemy had come out in massive force. A whistling slug tore through the fabric of his coat, another took the heel off his shoe. He charged into their ranks, the Beretta blasting with telling effect as the 9mm Parabellums spurted into the oppos-ing flashes, their success registering as despairing grunts and muffled cries.

Bolan was moving swiftly and feeling the Beretta a fresh clip when he collided with a large human bulk. They went down together in a sprawling tangle and a heavy weapon exploded almost in Bolan's face, the shot sizzling off into the night. Bolan's free hand chopped out and turned the weapon just as the hammer fell again and this time the shot buried itself in soft and unresisting flesh. The man wheezed, 'Oh, Jesus . . .' and melted fluidly out of the tangle.

Again Bolan rolled, getting as much distance as possible from that encounter. Running feet pounded toward him, shadowy shapes took form against a backdrop of sudden light. He came to one knee and sent all eight rounds of the new clip into that suddenly invisible pack. It scattered, with toppling bodies and shrieks of alarm.

The source of light was arching toward Bolan now: auto-mobile headlamps, blunted and haloed by the fog, and moving forward so that Bolan was not exposed to the full glare.

The enemy were either faltering or regrouping; there was silence and a sudden cessation of gunfire. Suddenly Bolan heard a feminine voice calling out to him, and it was coming from behind those headlamps. 'Bolan, get in!'

Another voice, harshly excited and far to the rear, yelled 'That car! Stop that car!'

The voice was American and Bolan thought that he had

15

heard it before but a new volley of fire, this one directed against the vehicle, was now commanding all his attention. The car was taking repeated hits and swerving erratically in tinkling glass when Bolan reached it. A door flew open and Bolan flew in, and was immediately pinned to the seat under high-G acceleration as the scene of carnage quickly fell behind.

Bolan had an impression of softly feminine curves, glistening dark hair worn short and casual, an almost luminous skin, a nice fragrance. He judged her to be about twenty-five, and scared half to death. A short skirt was crumpled high on the hips; gleaming thighs reflected the light from the dash; knee-high leather boots fit tight on well-turned calves that trembled almost out of control. The car whizzed in a tight circle around the railway station, then plunged down a narrow street. Somewhere off in the distance the wail of police vehicles was added to the insane quality of that soft misty night.

Bolan added a fresh clip of Parabellums to the pistol and told the girl, 'I'm grateful, but . . . that was a dumb stunt.'

She threw him a quick look, hardly more than a twitch of her eyes, and gasped, 'Don't speak of dumb stunts. Your odds back there were about thirty against one.'

'I was doing all right,' Bolan said quietly.

He recognized her suddenly, and also the car, a Jaguar sports model. He had noticed both aboard the ferry from Calais. He had even lit a cigarette for her on deck while they small-talked about the value of radar navigation through channel fog. Now he was hanging on grimly as the powerful vehicle swerved through the foggy streets, navigating without radar.

'You shall never get out of Dover unless you do exactly as I say,' she said in a voice thin with tension. 'The hatbox, behind you . . . it's yours, put it on quickly.'

'It' was a wig of fiery red hair and matching beard, also a seaman's jacket in Bolan's size. He stared at the contents of the box while his mind clicked through the various implications of this latest development. Obviously the rescue had been a planned, not a spontaneous, action.

Quickly the girl confirmed this. 'We'll exchange cars just

ahead,' she told him. 'Get into your hair and be ready for the jump.'

An uneasy feeling was crowding into Bolan's gut. Who the hell was the beautiful lady with the expensive car, and why was she interested in Mack Bolan's welfare? Where did she plan to take him, and for what purpose? From the noise of the sirens screaming through the night, it seemed that the police also had prepared some sort of reception for him. How had everyone tumbled so quickly to his movements? The idea of *manipulation* was churning in Bolan's mind, and he wondered just how prominently this lovely young woman had figured in those maneuvers.

At the moment, though, idle speculation was too great a luxury. His instinct told him to run with the play, and he was already reacting to the decision. The wig and false beard went on easily and snugly, and he was changing jackets when they braked to a squealing halt beside a waiting VW bus. A shadow figure moved forward immediately to take over the Jaguar; another was crouched over the steering wheel of the VW and impatiently gunning the motor. Bolan and the girl climbed quickly aboard the bus as the Jaguar disappeared into a small garage. A fast moving police vehicle with siren at full wail blasted out of the darkness to their rear and screamed past them.

The man in the driver's seat of the VW chuckled and moved the vehicle into the wake of the police car. The girl sat in a rear seat with Bolan. She breathed in quivering little gasps. She cuddled against him and, burying her face in his throat, she trembled with a hard case of the shakes.

Well, Bolan silently told himself, here we go again.

His chief interest in England had been as a link in his route back to the U.S., with possibly a quick hit on a couple of names in his notebook. But he had been required to fight his way into the country. Now, it appeared, he would have to fight his way out. No quick hits tonight. The jungle had closed in on him again, and he would have to hack his way through it.

His life had long ago become fixed in an unalterable groove, and Bolan had learned to accept the grim fact that everywhere he went became a battlefield. He had never,

17

however, thought too highly of a purely defensive mode of warfare. Particularly not against a massively superior enemy.

The girl was beginning to cry. He sighed and pulled her closer in a comforting embrace. He owed her a lot, whatever her motives. She'd pulled him out of a tough defensive position and now perhaps she was providing him with a temporary platform from which to launch a counter-offensive to carry him on through and out of England.

And not a bad platform, at that, he was thinking as the supple body molded against his. Down through history, he knew, lesser bodies had launched entire armadas and armies. What he did not know was that this one was fated to launch the Executioner's shattering assault upon Britain.

CHAPTER TWO

MUSEUM DE SADE

THE girl's nerves were in good shape. After a brief let-down, she dried her tears and regained her composure and was staring solemnly at Bolan's hands when the VW pulled into the lineup at the police blockade, just west of Dover. She pulled his arms around her, lay her head on his shoulder, and said 'Calmly now. Just let us do the talking. Don't give away your American accent.'

A uniformed officer stepped up to the driver's window and said something in a pleasant tone. The thick man at the wheel passed a paper through. The officer inspected it and handed it back, then held up something for the driver to look at. They conversed in low tones for a brief moment, then the policeman stepped down to the girl's window and lightly rapped his knuckles against it. She came out of the embrace slowly, reluctantly, then eyes going to the officer in a convincing display of confusion, as though she had just that moment become aware of the world outside.

The policeman touched his hat and passed in a large glossy photo of Bolan. 'Have you seen this chap?' he asked her.

She nodded her head immediately and replied, 'Many times, on the telly. It's that American adventurer.'

'Have you seen him tonight?'

She shook her head, confusion still very evident. Bolan shook his red-maned head also, growling something unintelligible in a guttural negative.

'Did you see a Jaguar sports roadster?'

The driver called back, 'You're wastin' yer time, Bob. Them two ain't seen nothin' this night but theirselves, I'll wager that.'

The young officer touched his hat, smiled faintly, and waved them through.

As they cleared the roadblock, the driver swiveled about to flash a grin at Bolan. 'And 'ow was that for 'andling the bloody situation, eh? We'll 'ave you in Londontown in no time now, mate. Just keep your pecker up.'

Slightly embarrassed by that last bit of advice, Bolan glanced at the girl.

She smiled and explained, 'He means that you should keep up your courage.'

Bolan grunted, let the girl go, and relaxed into the seat. He was going to have a language problem in England, perhaps more so than in France, this much was certain. But not immediately.

The balance of the trip was conducted in virtual silence, the girl withdrawing to her corner to gaze broodingly out the window, Boland silently scanning the road ahead and behind, and watching the movements of the driver. Explanations, he figured, would come in due course; he would play it step by step.

It was just past midnight when they entered London. They crossed the Thames at Westminster Bridge and swung up past Pall Mall to edge into the Soho district. Here the town was still very much awake, bustling with the after-theatre crowd and the people who swarmed the thousand and one restaurants, niteries, and discotheques which had established Soho as one of the mod capitals of the world.

Bolan was driven to a nineteenth century townhouse at the western edge of Soho, a handsome building with cut glass windows and a red carpeted entranceway. There was a simple metal plaque on the massive door.

Museum de Sade
Members Only

The VW dropped its passengers and drove away. Bolan followed the woman inside the building, seeing crystal chandeliers and dark wood. They went into a mahogany-paneled clubroom. The place was deserted, musty, oppressive. Bolan had a feeling of entombment.

He asked the girl, 'What kind of a museum is this?'

She flicked him a sidewise glance and murmured, 'It's private. No worry, I'm the curator. My name is Ann Franklin.'

'Why did you bring me here?'

She replied, 'It isn't my place to tell you that. Please be comfortable while I ring up the directors.'

'What directors?' he asked.

'The directors of the museum. It is they who arranged all this, though I must say we didn't expect the fireworks at Dover.' The girl was moving away from him, toward a door at the far side of the room. 'The bar is over there,' she called back, pointing it out with a flourish. 'Please be comfortable.'

Bolan felt not at all comfortable. He removed the false hair and beard and changed back into his own jacket. Then he went to the bar, poured some tonic into a glass, and tasted it before he went to try the door through which the girl had gone but his suspicions were confirmed, it was locked. He retraced his steps across the room and tried the other door. It, too, was locked.

Uneasily and with a growing sense of alarm, Bolan returned to the bar. He lit a cigarette and caught a flash of something reflecting off the opposite wall as he extinguished the flame of his lighter. Closer investigation revealed a wide-angle camera lens set flush into the paneling. He glared at it for a moment, then placed a hand over the lens and called out, 'Okay, end of game. What's going on here?'

A cultured and crisply British voice responded immediately through a speaker concealed somewhere overhead. 'You are quite perceptive, Mr. Bolan. Welcome to England. We hope you'll like us here. Dreadfully sorry for all that bother at Dover, you know. Please understand that we had nothing at all to do with that.'

Bolan let his hand fall away from the wall and he stepped back to gaze coldly into the lens. 'Shades of James Bond,' he said drily. 'Locked room, closed circuit television, the whole bit. What's it all about?'

A short, barking laugh preceded, 'Surely you will understand our caution, Mr. Bolan. Your reputation is ah, legendary to say the least. We think it best that—'

Bolan angrily interrupted with, 'No way, friend. Either those doors come open in twenty seconds or I'm blasting out.'

A brief pause, then: 'Please don't be boorish, Mr. Bolan. Nor imprudent. As soon as Miss Franklin completes her report then we'll see what can be done.'

'Boorish, hell,' Bolan said. He sprung the Beretta and put a bullet through the camera lens. The report of the gun, magnified, reverberated in the tightly closed room.

'Really, Mr. Bolan . . .' the voice spluttered.

Calmly Bolan asked, 'Can you still see me?'

'Of course not, sir. You have just sent a shot directly into the camera.'

'So now we're even,' Bolan replied. 'You have about ten seconds to get those doors open.'

'That's impossible,' was the angry retort. 'Be reasonable, man. We can't just—'

Bolan snapped. 'Time's up.' He went to the door through which the girl had disappeared and shot the lock off, then pushed into a small cell-like room and on through into a larger area with oriental rugs and tapestries. There were no windows. Low couches and harem pillows were scattered about. The aromatic sweetness of some exotic incense hung lightly in the atmosphere. A large arched doorway at the far side of the room drew Bolan's attention. It was framed by a huge woodcarving of shapely buttocks, through which could be viewed unmistakable cherrywood labia standing taller than Bolan and serving as the actual doorway.

'Some museum,' Boland muttered, and stepped cautiously through the parted labia. He found himself on a narrow, darkened stairway which led steeply to an upper floor. Slowly he ascended, the Beretta ready, and exited into another cell-like room. It had an unvarnished wooden floor and was bare except for a small desk and several folding chairs. Suspended from a peg on the wall was an ancient iron chastity belt, of the type used by knights of the crusades to keep their ladies securely chaste during their extended absences during the holy wars.

Bolan sniffed and went on through to another cubicle, this one dimly lighted by a bare bulb in the ceiling. It contained nothing but a narrow wooden cot, obviously very old. The head and foot boards were actually stocks for imprisoning the hands and feet in a widespread position.

A trickling chill of revulsion traversed Bolan's spine. He was beginning to understand just what sort of museum this was. The next cubicle confirmed his suspicions. It was totally bare except for a pair of wrist-irons set high into the wall. On the floor beneath the irons was a small barrel with a narrow board placed across it. The use was obvious. The 'victim' would be forced to balance on the unstable platform or else suffer his entire weight dangling from the harsh irons at his wrists.

A large black whip was coiled about a peg on the opposite wall. Bolan found himself visualizing some miserable wretch trying to maintain a foothold on the barrel with that cat o' nine flaying into his naked flesh. The museum's name tied in neatly then. Bolan was not overly sophisticated in matters of kinky sex but he knew of the Marquis de Sade, one of the most famous writers of forbidden literature and the man from whose name the term *sadism* was coined.

Bolan shivered and moved on out of there and through a succession of similar cubicles containing various of the diabolical torture devices. He was beginning to feel as though he were trapped in a maze when he finally got to another stairway and ascended to still another floor and found a neat duplicate of the clubroom below. Ann Franklin was standing near a small desk. She stared at him over the mouthpiece of a telephone. He told her, 'Hang up.'

She did so without argument, looking at the pistol in his hand. 'You're behaving badly,' she said, calmly. 'We are only trying to help.'

'Maybe you're trying too hard,' he told her, moving around the room to study it. 'I'm not here to play games. Where's the guy?'

'Which guy?' she asked quietly.

'The guy with the brigadier's voice and a peeping Tom's manners. Where was he talking from?'

'Oh . . . so you discovered that.'

'Sure I discovered it.' Bolan had completed his reconnaissance of the room and ended his search at the girl's side.

The Beretta went back into the sideleather and he told her, 'Well, I appreciate the ride into town. Is there a quicker way out of here other than through the chamber of horrors?'

'But you can't leave now,' she protested weakly.

'The hell I can't.' His voice softened as he added, 'Look, you did a gutsy thing down there at Dover, and I'm indebted to you. But I didn't invite you in, you know, and gratitude can stretch just so far. For openers, it won't cover being locked up in a house of sick sex and watched with a hidden camera.'

The girl's eyes fell. She said, 'Sorry about the security. It *is* necessary, you know. I mean, don't imagine that we installed all that expressly for your benefit. If you're wondering about Charles, he's in the cellar, the security station. But don't please go down there bothering him. He's a nice old love who wouldn't harm a flea.'

Bolan said, 'This is more than just a museum, isn't it?'

'Of course.' Her eyes met his, almost defiantly he thought. 'Every one has a right to sex, even if their outlets are ... limited. We provide that outlet here, at *de Sade*.'

'With whips and racks,' he observed drily.

'Oh, those are just props. Psychological, you know. Our members are not psychotics. Their need is for ... stimulative fantasy. It's rather like pornography.'

'I see,' Bolan said. 'A trip through the maze of horrors and they're ready to swing, eh? Come on now, that doesn't even make sense.'

'We have ... a paid staff,' she explained in a small voice. 'Certain ... stimulating services ... may be purchased.'

Bolan decided the girl was trying to delay him, to keep him there. Until what? He told her, 'Well, that's none of my business. Who are we expecting?'

'What?'

'You're trying to keep me here until someone else arrives. Who?'

She said, 'I told you earlier that I had to ring up the directors.'

'What's their interest in me?'

'Permit them to tell you that.'

'No. You tell me. Right now, or I'm walking.'

'They want to help you.'

'Why?'

She moved her shoulders delicately and replied, 'They want you to help them, also. But I shouldn't be discussing this, really. You must wait and let them tell you.'

'Tell me what?'

Her hip swung into contact with his thigh. She quickly jerked it back and laughed nervously, resting a hand on his shoulder. 'You Americans can look so fierce and frightening,' she said.

'Do I frighten you?'

'Of course.' Her other arm went up and she pressed full against him with a soft little sigh, then pushed herself regretfully away and turned her back to him. 'All right,' she said. 'Go on. Start walking. I couldn't blame you for that.'

Bolan watched her for a moment, trying to read her. Such a lovely thing . . . what part did she play in the nutty goings-on at this house of kinks? He sighed, deciding there would be too much involvement there for a guy bent on blitzing through.

'Thanks for Dover,' he muttered, and moved quickly toward the door.

A man stood there, blocking the way out, a Hollywood casting director's idea of a retired British military officer, complete to tidy little moustache and stiff tweed suit. The hair was combed straight back, thin and streaked with gray, and the stiffly erect posture made him appear much taller than his five seven or eight.

Bolan's hand moved inside his jacket and he said, 'Well, here's Charlie.'

'Wrong,' the man snapped. 'Charles is busy replacing a very expensive camera which you destroyed for no reason. Really, Bolan, that was a beastly reaction to an offer of friendship.'

Bolan replied, 'Friends don't lock me up.' The Beretta was in his hand and he was moving toward the doorway again.

The little man stood his ground, blocking the exit.

'There's no time to explain all that now. The point is, Bolan, that you cannot possibly leave here now. You'll walk onto that street to certain death. Our mutual enemy is out there in force, waiting for you to show.'

'How do you know that?'

'I saw them as I was coming here. The entire square is sealed off.'

Uneasily, Bolan asked, 'Just who are you talking about? The police?'

'Of course not, though I imagine they're not too far off either.'

Bolan sighed. 'You said "mutual enemy". Explain.'

'The same people who want you are trying to destroy *us* in quite a different fashion. We helped you get into England, you know. We thought—'

'Okay, that explains one small mystery,' Bolan interrupted. 'But Dover was also swarming with *Mafiosi*. How did they know?'

'Yes, well, that bothers us also, you know. Security leak somewhere, no doubt. Never worry we shall find it.'

'I'll buy that for now,' Bolan told him. 'So what does my presence here mean to you? An executioner for your side?'

The man shrugged his shoulders. 'That's putting it rather bluntly but ... yes, I suppose that's it. You're dedicated to the extinction of certain elements. We have them here, you know, right here in London. We decided ... well, we took the vote, Bolan.'

'What vote?'

'We decided to sponsor you for a stay in London.'

'I'm not for hire,' Bolan quietly replied.

'Of course not,' the man said quickly. 'I did not mean to suggest ... we offer you only cooperation.'

'What sort of cooperation?'

'We'll provide you with intelligence, and protect you in every possible way.'

Bolan was thinking it over.

'And,' the man continued, 'when you've finished here, we will help you safely out of the country.'

Bolan had reached his decision.

'No deal,' he reported, in a tone which left no hope for negotiation. 'Now stand aside. I'm leaving.'

A strained smile pulled at the man's lips. 'Kipling's cat,' he said musingly.

'What?'

'I was thinking of one of Rudyard Kipling's stories, about a jungle cat. "He went back through the wet wild woods, waving his wild tail, and walking by his wild lone." That's you, Bolan, a wild jungle beast that walks by himself. Quite admirable, really. I'll see that it's carved onto your burial stone.'

Bolan said, 'Thanks.' He jostled the man aside and passed on to the stairway.

The girl cried out, 'Wait!' and hurried after him. She overtook him at the bottom step and pressed a key into his hand. 'Queen's House,' she whispered, 'front flat, upper. Across from the park on Russell Square. You'll find it easily. It's safe there, and you're welcome any time.'

Bolan kissed her forehead, murmured 'Okay,' and went on. The key went into his pocket, though a flat on Russell Square seemed the remotest of all possibilities for him at the moment. If the stiff little man had not been trying to con him, a street full of *Mafiosi* awaited him just outside. He took a deep breath and checked the load in the Beretta.

The cat that walked by himself, eh? Bolan grinned faintly to himself and fingered his spare clips: he liked that. He was going out there to wave his wild tail through those wet wild Mafia woods, and that was okay. Bolan had learned jungle law and how to live by it. All jungles were alike; the same law operated through them all. Kill quick and hard, then fade to return and do it again. Bolan knew the law. It was older than mankind, older than men's laws. And Bolan himself could quote a bit of Kipling.

'Now this is the Law of the Jungle – as old and as true as the sky.'

Or how about, 'Through the Jungle very softly flits a shadow and a sigh – He is Fear, O Little Hunter, he is Fear!'

Yeah, Bolan decided, Kipling had been there too.

He went back through the grim little cells of the second floor and down through the carved labia and spreading buttocks into the harem room. This trip through he noticed the phallic statuary, vases shaped like leather hipboots, lamp-shades made to look like corsets, and various other items of erotic decor. He shook his head sadly thinking of the girl upstairs, and passed quickly on through to the clubroom.

Then he found an elderly man kneeling beside an open panel of the wall. The man looked up with a frown at Bolan's entry, then averted his eyes from the fierce encounter.

Bolan commanded, 'Show me a quiet way out.'

Charles heaved to his feet and said, 'Down through the cellar is the best way, but it'll only deposit you just across the square. I'd call it a very tiny advantage.'

'Fine,' Bolan said. It was all he needed, one tiny advantage. He'd make it stretch all the way through the wet wild woods.

CHAPTER THREE

DEATH IN THE SPOT

CHARLES, it developed, was his family name. The given name was Edwin but he preferred to be called Charles. Per Bolan's earlier voice judgement, he was indeed a former army officer – *twice* retired he was quick to point out. During World War Two, Charles had been a high-ranking staff officer in liaison with the American cloak and dagger outfit, OSS. He'd grown to know the Americans quite well, admired them, and jolly well understood and admired Bolan's quick reaction to 'the security watch' at *de Sade*.

Bolan would have had a tough time judging the old man's age; he hung it in at about seventy-five, realizing that he could be five years off in either direction. Judging purely by mental spryness, Bolan would have scaled down the years considerably. Charles was alert and quick, with plenty of fire remaining behind the old eyes. Only the physical gave away his age, and even here only in his movements, for he was tall and straight, slim without appearing bony. He had once been a very powerful man, Bolan guessed. His jaw was long and hard, he was clean-shaven, his hair was thick and wavy, though snowy white. Bolan decided he would have liked to know Charles thirty or forty years before.

The escape route from *de Sade* had been a sewer at some time in ages past. Charles accompanied Bolan out, proudly pointing out places where they had 'restructured' around WW2 bomb damage to keep the old tunnel passable. Not too many years earlier, he added, a secret route of escape from the town house had been a must; now the tunnel was regarded as just another museum piece to be carefully preserved, as a link to the past.

'Anything goes in London these days,' the old man told

Bolan, his eyes twinkling. 'Rather takes the fun out of sin, what?'

When they arrived at the other end, Bolan thanked him, delivered an offhand apology for the shattered television camera, then he climbed an iron ladder and lifted himself to the surface.

Charles, his face dimly illumined in the side glow of a pocket flashlight, was peering up at him with considerable anxiety. 'Remember to look before you leap, Yank,' he called up.

Grinning, Bolan replied, 'Okay, I'll remember that, Brigadier.'

'This crackling museum of ours. You should realize that it has a deeper meaning, quite aside from its obvious purpose. It's a symbol of *our* times, Bolan. Remember that. *Our* times.'

Bolan's grin faded. He gave a curt wave and lowered the door on the concerned face. What, he wondered, prompted a grand old man like this into such questionable activities? He should be sitting out his days in a quiet clubroom somewhere, recounting the glories of days gone by. Instead, he played Secret Agent at a house of kinks.

Bolan shook Charles out of his mind and took up the problem at hand. He was in the basement of another building situated directly opposite the *Museum de Sade*. The Sades operated this establishment, too. It was a book store and sexprop shop. A dim yellow bulb revealed the basement was a storeroom, with cartons of merchandise stacked about rather haphazardly. Bolan went up the flight of rickety stairs, found a key where Charles had assured him he would, and let himself into the shop. Here was utter darkness, except for a limited penetration of street light through the windows up front.

Bolan moved quietly to the edge of darkness and took up a patient surveillance of the activities outside. The fog was gone, except as a faintly visible pall hanging just above the rooftops. A half-dozen regularly spaced street lamps broke the darkness here and there about the square without actually relieving it. After several minutes of watchful waiting, someone just outside the shop but out of Bolan's range of vision lit a cigarette. Bolan saw the glow from the match and seconds later a puff of smoke drifting past the window. The guy was close.

Some minutes later a large car cruised past, moving slowly. It was an American make, quickly identified by Bolan as a Lincoln. Four, perhaps five persons were inside. Bolan's attention was drawn to a large spotlight mounted on the driver's side. These boys were a hunting party.

Shortly after the vehicle moved out of view, a man sauntered into the light of a street lamp across the way, seemed to consult a wrist watch, then he too faded into the darkness.

Yeah, it was a hard set.

The Lincoln returned some moments later and halted on Bolan's side of the square, out of his field of vision. A large man with thick shoulders immediately strolled past the shop, barely ten feet from Bolan's position, and disappeared in the direction of the vehicle. Almost at the same moment, the door opened at the *Museum de Sade* and Ann Franklin came out. Bolan watched her tensely, wondering about her reception by those waiting in the street. She crossed the traffic circle and halted in the small park at the center, standing beneath a street lamp. She seemed to be looking toward the bookshop; Charles had told her, no doubt, of Bolan's mode of exit.

Bolan fidgeted and watched the girl. What the hell was she trying to do? As he watched, a man came out of the darkness walking directly toward the girl. He made a close pass and went on by. Ann swiveling to watch him out of sight. Had they spoken? Bolan could not tell; it had appeared not.

Seconds later a taxicab eased into the circle and halted alongside the girl. She entered and the cab went on. A moment later another vehicle which Bolan had not seen earlier swung into view and circled around to fall in behind the taxi.

No, she had not spoken. They'd made an identity pass, pulled the make, and were now following her. They were missing no bets.

Nor was Bolan. His quiet surveillance had gained him a rather valid impression of the terrain out there, and of the forces arrayed against him. It was a mighty hard set, too hard for any ideas of a frontal assault. So, once again, Bolan's time had come.

He went back through the shop and let himself out through the rear entrance. The alleyway was narrow, smelly, and densely dark, running along the side of the shop and dead-ending a few feet to the rear. Bolan took the only way out, moving cautiously toward the square, and rounded the corner in a casual stroll. The big man he had noted earlier outside the shop was now standing just downrange, leaning against a building about half-way between the shop and the Lincoln, arms folded across his chest in a stance of tired boredom. He did not see Bolan until they were in an almost direct confrontation, then he started visibly and whispered, 'Shit, don't come up like that. You scared the—'

Bolan told him, 'Relax. I don't think the guy's over there. I think it's a bum stand.' He edged in close to the man, keeping a distant street lamp behind him.

'Is that what Danno thinks?'

'Yeh,' Bolan replied. His mind was clicking out the name. *Danno Giliamo?* Could be. A lieutenant in a New Jersey mob. Bolan probed. 'Jersey was never like this, eh,' he said disgustedly.

'Any place is like this at two in th' morning,' the man replied. He was showing an interest in Bolan's face and having a bad time at identification in the London blackness.

Probably, Bolan guessed, wondering about rank. People in the mob were very rank conscious. Bolan pushed his advantage. 'Go on over and get some coffee,' he commanded gruffly.

'They got coffee over there?'

'I *said* coffee, didn't I?'

The man sighed, mumbled something disparaging about 'English coffee', and dug in his pocket for a cigarette. Bolan slapped the pack out of his hand, snarling, 'Whatta you, nuts? You don't go lighting no fires out here!'

'You said it was a bum stand,' the man replied quietly. He retrieved the cigarettes and dropped them into a pocket. 'Look,' he added, 'I didn't come all the way over here for a cup of lousy coffee. I want a shot at that hundred thou. Now if the guy ain't here, then I say let's go find out where he's at.'

A contract man, Bolan thought. Bounty hunter, twentieth century style. Not even in the mob, but a freelancer. This intelligence opened interesting possibilities. Bolan pushed a step further.

'What's your name again?' he growled.

'Dunlap,' the big man replied defiantly. 'Jack Dunlap. You want me to spell it?'

'Just don't forget, Jack Dunlap,' Bolan said, playing for all the marbles now, 'that Danno and me are standing your expenses.' He chuckled drily. 'I like a hot-trotter. You get over there and have yourself some coffee. And you tell Danno that Frankie says you get a spot up front. Understand? Where the action is. Eh?'

The man was grinning. He said, 'Sure, Frankie. You won't be sorry. What I hit stays hit, you'll see.'

'Just save enough to identify, eh?'

'Sure.' Dunlap chuckled. 'I go for the gut, so I hope you don't identify by belly buttons.' He made one last futile attempt to get a good look at Bolan's face, then moved on out and started across the street.

Bolan immediately glided down to the Lincoln which was idling at the curb just downrange, lights out, engine running. A stir of interest inside the vehicle greeted his approach. He bent down to speak through the driver's window and snapped, 'You boys get out there and cover Dunlap. He's spotted something.'

Three doors opened instantly and quiet feet began moving off into the darkness. The driver remained in his seat. Bolan swung the door open and snarled, 'You too, dammit, get out there!'

The man leapt out and ran quietly after the others. Bolan leaned inside and found the control lever for the spotlight. An instant later a brilliant beam stabbed across the darkness of the square and picked up the sauntering figure of Jack Dunlap.

Bolan roared, 'There he is!'

Dunlap froze for an instant when the beam hit him, then he spun about with a large revolver in his hand and tried to dive out of the sudden brilliance. Others reacted quicker, and a hail of fire swept the spot, jerking the man about like a rag doll and punching him to the ground.

Bolan was behind the wheel and easing the car forward. *'Wrong guy!'* he yelled, and the spot picked up another figure running in from the far side of the square. This one halted stockstill and thrust his hands high overhead.

'Not me!' he screeched as another rattling volley descended, and sieved him, and flung him into eternity.

Bolan had the vehicle moving swiftly now, out into the traffic circle with all lights extinguished, and angling toward a broad exit. Sporadic bursts of gunfire continued to disrupt the stillness of the night and an excited voice over near the *Museum de Sade* was loudly demanding a ceasefire.

Bolan opened the big car up going into the turn. A gun crew at the corner gaped at him as he roared past, but no shots followed him. Apparently the confusion was complete.

Allies, Bolan was thinking, should at least know each other. They should, also, know their enemy.

This was an admonition which the Executioner would have cause to remember later. For the moment, he was free and running through the wet wild woods of London-town.

CHAPTER FOUR

THE CLOSING JUNGLE

DANNO GILIAMO was a mighty unhappy man. Twice in one night he had set a flawless trap for that Bolan bastard, and twice in one night the bastard had skipped lightly away and left a pile of bleeding bodies behind him.

'The trouble,' Danno complained to his local contact, 'is that I'm trying to do a job with nothing but a bunch of two-bit amateurs. We're never going to nail that guy with this kind of talent.'

Nick Trigger, a powerfully built man about forty-five, thoughtfully chewed the end of an unlighted cigar, and studied the troubled *caporegime* from Jersey. Known earlier by various names – Endante, Fumerri, Woods, to list only the most recent – Nick had been a trigger man with various eastern mobs since the late forties. He had come to England less than a year earlier, with false papers and under the name Nicholas Woods, and with a singular mission to perform for the council of bosses back home in the U.S. In coded communications travelling between the two countries, this veteran triggerman was identified as Nick Trigger, and the code name had stuck.

Nick's mission in England was true to his trade. He had been commissioned to discourage organized competition with the mob's British arm during their entrenchment there. A better man for the task could hardly have been chosen. Tough, tenacious, highly intelligent and coldly merciless, he is thought to have figured directly or indirectly in more than a hundred Mafia executions during his criminal career. Many of these victims had formerly been close associates.

Now, as Nick Trigger, this same assassin was chief British

35

enforcer for the Council of Capo's, reporting directly to the *Commissione* – and he was not entirely happy with the untidy bundle being edged into his lap by the man from Jersey. He pulled the cigar from his mouth and quietly asked his visitor, 'How many boys you running with, Danno?'

Nervously, Giliamo replied, 'I brought a dozen of my personal crew, and now two of them are hurt. I got about twenty freelancers left, ones I brought with me. Local talent I never know about, it keeps varying. For every one that gets shot, I lose ten to the trembling shakes.'

'Well how many locals you think you got right now?'

'I think maybe a couple dozen.'

Trigger whistled softly. 'Hell, you got a regular army. You can't nail Bolan with all that?'

'You gotta see this guy to believe it,' Giliamo said. 'It ain't numbers that's going to get him, it's talent. Now I got some pretty damn good boys with me, Nick, but I ain't got any in *that* bastard's league. As for these tagalong rodmen, it's almost criminal neglect to even put them on the firing line. This Bolan just whacks 'em down and sends for some more. You ought to see what he did to us on this last hit, and I bet he didn't fire a shot himself. He had my boys shootin' *each other* up.'

'He's pretty tricky, eh?'

'Cunning is the word, Nick. This fuckin' boy is *cunning*.'

Nick Trigger chewed his cigar for another thoughtful moment, then asked, 'Just what is it you want from me, Danno?'

'I thought maybe you'd like to take it over, Nick.'

'This Bolan hit?'

'Yeah. I don't know anybody else off hand could handle this job except Nick Trigger.'

'I hear he put down the Talifero brothers in Miami,' the other murmured.

'Hard, he put them down *damn* hard, that's right. I was there. I saw it. Not just the brothers got put down. The whole place was a disaster area.'

'The Talifero's are about the two meanest boys around

anywhere,' Nick Trigger observed, sighing. 'What the hell, maybe this boy Bolan is as big as his reputation.'

'He is, Nick,' Giliamo quickly affirmed. 'Bigger maybe. He scares the living shit outta my boys, I gotta be honest about that. They're so jittery and keyed-up they start shooting holes in each other if anything moves. I gotta be honest about this. I don't know anybody could take this boy except maybe you.'

The veteran triggerman smiled grimly. 'Don't try buttering me up, Danno. I don't take jobs on butter.'

'I'm just being honest,' Giliamo assured him. 'You know I'm just being honest, Nick.'

'Yeah.' Trigger was thinking about it. 'I been walking a thin line here in England, you know. I mean, a lot's at stake and we don't have things nailed down too good. I have a hell of a big job without all this other trouble.'

'I know, Nick, I know. I was just thinking that . . .'

'We got a lot of legit money invested around. Hell we got movie companies and theatres, clubs, casinos – hell, we got a lot of money strung out around here, Danno. We even have musical groups and records and that kind of stuff. And it's tight – the competish is tight. Nobody's on the make in this town, neither. I mean the cops, the government people – they don't have any handle to grab hold of. I never saw such an honest damn country as this one.'

'I understood you wasn't involved in the business end of things,' Giliamo said. 'I mean, you're enforcing, right?'

'Yeah you're right, Danno, but what I'm saying is all this makes my job tougher. If you can't buy security then you got to *take* it – right? I mean, hell, if the local biggies won't co-operate then you have to carve out a territory the best way you can. And that means I'm busier'n hell, Danno.'

'Well, I figure you could handle this job just one two three, Nick. And it would be a real feather in your cap. I mean, you know, it'd show everybody once and for all that you're two heads bigger than the Talifero boys. Right,'

Nick Trigger let out a tired sigh. He plucked at his tie and pushed a coffee cup in little circles about the table. 'I'd have to clear it with the people back home,' he said.

'That wouldn't be any trouble,' Giliamo assured him. 'They want Bolan more'n they want Manhattan. I'd appreciate it, though, if you'd put it in a way that wouldn't make me look like an ass. You know. Just tell 'em I don't know the town or something, and you'd like to take over and get this Bolan out of your hair real quick. You know. Don't make it look like I'm flat on my ass.'

'Yeah, well, what you say is true, Danno.' Trigger told him. 'Many more open gunfights around here and the whole town will pull up tight. I don't see the C.I.D. swarming around my operation. Those boys are bad news all the way.'

'What's that C.I.D.?' asked the man from Jersey.

'That's what Scotland Yard calls their dick force, Crimininal Investigation Division. They're worse news than the feds back home.'

'So that's what you tell 'em,' Giliamo quickly replied. 'Tell 'em you want to take over, and that I'll stick around to help out.'

'Okay. Let me think about it,' the British enforcer said quietly. But he had already thought about it. Bolan would be a real plum, and at just about the right time. Nick Trigger had the British territory in much better shape than he'd let on to Danno Giliamo. Pretty soon he'd be needing to move onward and upward. And it wouldn't hurt a thing to come home looking two heads bigger than the Talifero brothers. Hell no, it wouldn't hurt a thing.

In an imposing building beside the Thames a group of grim faced men were sitting down to a new day with a rather large sized new problem confronting them. They were solemn, some sleepy and obviously newly awake. There was a minimum of conversation. The time was barely four o'clock.

Their leader stood stiffly in front of a wall chart of the city of London, his arms folded against his chest, and waited until all had been seated and the subdued greetings quietly exchanged. Then he dropped his arms to his side, advanced a couple of steps to a small rostrum, fiddled with a paper lying there, and said, 'Well, it's a brisk hour to be starting the

38

day, isn't it? I can see that we're all fired up and anxious to be cracking along, so I'll make this as brief as possible.'

He paused, as though expecting some reaction to his dry humor. Receiving none, he plunged right in. 'It's this chap Bolan, the American answer to overpopulation. We have good reason to believe that he entered this country at Dover late last night.'

He received his reaction then. Sleepy eyes suddenly became wide-awake, a fellow at the rear closed his mouth in mid-yawn, others exchanged significant glances which meant that a rumor had just been confirmed.

'So you can understand the early hour call. There's much to be done and not nearly enough time, we fear, to get it all in. Please listen alertly, take notes, question anything that isn't crystal clear to you. Very quickly now, here are the facts as known at this ...'

The meeting took forty minutes and revealed the full scope of Scotland Yard's reaction to the Bolan presence in England. All routine police business had been temporarily suspended, all furloughs indefinitely cancelled, shift rotations halted, and the full force of the most impressive police establishment in existence brought to bear directly upon the problem of Mack Bolan.

It was an extraordinary reaction, but a carefully considered one. Bolan's presence in France, and the resulting uproar there, had been closely noted by the men this side of the channel. The chance that Bolan would come to England had been weighed as a fifty-fifty question, and a rather thin security screen had been set up at all likely points of entry. Bolan had slipped in and in the space of a few hours two explosive and widely separated gun battles had erupted.

Contingency plans had been drawn up at Scotland Yard some days earlier, ready to be put into operation at a moment's notice. Already the machinery was in motion, the inexorable gears of British crime control meshing into the problem. Special squads were activated, undercover contacts alerted, and hot lines opened to underworld informers all about the city. All public transportation terminals were placed under close surveillance, car rental and taxicab companies were alerted, and a watch was established on all persons known or suspected to have connections with organized crime.

The battle for Britain was on, and the Executioner's jungle was again closing in on him.

CHAPTER FIVE

THE RUNNING TIDE

BOLAN had definitely not desired a hot war in London. He knew neither the land nor the people, and his intelligence concerning local Mafia activities was practically nil. There were several names in his target book, and that was all: he had no addresses, no rundown of activities, no feel whatever about the enemy. The only logical course of action that presented itself to him was to get the hell away from there, and with as little lost motion as possible. His intention upon his departure from France, had been to skim through England and quickly out again, U.S. bound. This initiative had been taken away from him, though, with the appearance of Ann Franklin into his life. For the moment, he had felt it best to run with the tide – and he had done so.

The brief skirmish outside the *Museum de Sade* was now more than an hour behind him. He had been running loose since that time with no particular objective in mind except to keep moving. He had driven aimlessly, winding and circling through the maze-like metropolis while considering alternate plans of action.

Ann Franklin and old Charles kept crowding into his mind, along with the cocky little rooster who'd stood unarmed in his path in that upstairs clubroom and the anonymous men who had helped him out of Dover and through the police lines into London. *Why?* Why all of it? Why *any* of it? The lengths they had gone to, all the planning and intrigue and personal danger . . . what manner of peril had prompted them into such a hazardous undertaking?

Bolan was feeling guilty about his treatment of the people of the *de Sade*. He recognized this, and attempted to combat the feeling with logic. Regardless of their motives, he argued, few things could be more perilous than an alignment with Mack Bolan. Recent history substantiated this conclusion. Everyone who had held out a hand of friendship to the Executioner had gotten that hand promptly chopped off, in one way or another. The Mafia did not take kindly to active sympathy for their enemies. Bolan's list of beloved dead stretched all the way back to the California battles, and hovered on his conscience like an open wound. And in France he had damn near . . .

He wrenched off the thought and flung it away. The Executioner could not afford the luxury of mourning. Following that heart-rending action in France, Bolan had sworn to never again allow himself any involvements with friendly units. And now he was reaffirming that position; he would not involve the *Sades*.

Case closed.

Next problem, get out of London. This could be no easy chore in a 'hot' vehicle, especially a big foreign job that stood out like a neon sign.

As an additional complication, Bolan was lost. The appropriated car had come complete with a street map of the city, but only principal thoroughfares and notable landmarks were shown. Since his discovery of the map, Bolan had found nothing to offer him an orientation to the lay of the city and his relative position in the sprawling confusion.

After several minutes of travelling the maze, however, he came out on a broad avenue and shortly thereafter passed a planetarium and Madame Tussaud's waxworks. Now Bolan had his fix. He was on Marylebone Road, just south of Regent's Park and Zoological Gardens.

He swung into the park and stopped the car to study the map and develop some logic of the London layout. He was far north and a bit west of center. London Airport lay south and even further west. He quickly traced a street route between the two points; then, on impulse, he got out of the car and went back to inspect the trunk compartment.

As soon as he looked in Bolan knew that he had gained far more than a set of wheels; he'd inherited an arsenal. The trunk was crammed with weapons – among them a sawed-off shotgun, an efficient little Israeli *Uzi* submachinegun, and an impressive high-powered bolt action piece, a Weatherby Mark V with a sniperscope and about fifty rounds of .460 Magnum heartstoppers. This last find evoked a low whistle from the arms expert. It came in a leather case which may have cost as much as the rifle itself; the gun was loaded and ready to roar, and it had been sighted-in with calibrations up to 1,000 yards. In a pocket of the guncase Bolan found a trajectory graph and a ballistics chart. This drew another appreciative response. According to the graph, trajectory drop was less than five inches at maximum calibrated range, and the point-blank range (no correction required) was a little better than 400 yards.

The Weatherby was a precision piece, and it had been further refined by a real craftsman. Bolan was not only happy to have the gun – he was damned glad that an enemy no longer had it. Anyone who could work-in a rifle like that would certainly know how to make the proper use of it. This item of knowledge also sharpened the Executioner's respect for the enemy. All were not clowns; some were masters of death, and the Weatherby served to remind him of this grim fact.

Now he had cause for wonder about the big Lincoln and its proposed role in the British squeeze on Bolan. These gunners had obviously come loaded for bear, and it seemed unlikely that a couple of brief firefights would deter them from their hunt.

Bolan re-secured the weapons in the trunk and sent the car along to his next point of reference, the intersection of Marylebone Road and Baker Street, then along Baker to Oxford and over to the broad Park Lane at the eastern edge of Hyde Park. He passed the London-Hilton and circled to Knightsbridge, then began angling towards Cromwell Road and London Airport.

His first port o' call would be the air express terminal to pick up the bag he had sent ahead from Paris. It contained items he could use immediately – such as a change of suits and a pair of shoes with both heels intact. There were also some special cosmetics he'd picked up in a shop at Marseilles which might prove beneficial.

As for the weapons now in the trunk of the Lincoln, Bolan

had already written them off. If things worked out right he would not and could not make any use of them – Bolan was fading, not charging. There was a twinge of regret over the Weatherby. As for the other stuff, general weapons could be picked up anywhere, when and as the need arose. For the moment, the Beretta was weapon enough.

London Airport presented itself as a confusing sprawl. Overseas flights used one terminal, intra-European flights another. To complicate matters, the road signs directing traffic into the complex could have meant as much to Bolan if printed in Singhalese, and the fog was much worse in this area. After some twenty minutes of trial and error, he found his way to the freight terminal. Then he devoted another ten minutes to a soft recon of that part of the airpark. When finally he went inside to claim the bag. Bolan knew all the ways in and out and the Lincoln was ready for an unobstructed departure.

His business at the express office was conducted quickly and without difficulty. The customs formalities had been taken care of at the shipping point, and Bolan identified himself with a fake American passport he had purchased in Paris. He returned to the car and deposited the bag on the rear seat, then set off for the overseas passenger area. Here he parked in a zone reserved for buses from the BOAC Air Terminal in London, grabbed the bag, and walked briskly toward the flight facility.

When he was within a few yards of his goal hurrying footsteps sounded at his side and a strained emotional voice advised him, 'You mustn't go in there, Mr. Bolan.'

Ann Franklin, it seemed, was not yet entirely out of his life.

She was compellingly appealing in a London Fog minicoat, a jaunty little hat, and a very worried face. Bolan's hand slipped inside his jacket, and he growled, 'Why not?'

'Charles thought you'd wish to know,' she reported breathlessly. 'The C.I.D. is out in force, searching for you. Here too. Charles says there will be an undercover man at each booking stall.'

'At each what?'

'The ticketing windows – the places where you purchase
... never mind, you simply cannot get out this way.'

Bolan's decision was typically quick. He took the girl by
the arm and returned to the parked car, put her and the bag
inside, then slid in behind the wheel and quietly departed.

When they were clear of the airport proper he said,
'Thanks again. But just how clean are you?'

'What?'

'You left the museum with a Mafia tail.'

'Oh, that.' She gave the lovely head a disdainful toss. 'I
left them chasing their own tails around Piccadilly.'

Bolan turned her a warm grin. 'You're something else,' he
said in a quietly respectful tone.

'In American, I hope that's good,' she replied, smiling.

'Yeah, it is.' He sighed and added, 'How long have you
been standing out in the cold waiting for me?'

'Not long,' she assured him. 'We weren't all that certain
that you hadn't slipped out before Charles rung me at just
past four. I came straight out. Major Stone took the
B.O.A.C. Terminal. Harry Parks, that's the large one who
chauffeured us into London – Harry went to intercept you at
the West London Terminal.' She laughed nervously. 'I think
it perfectly fitting that I drew the lucky spot.'

Drily, Bolan said, 'Yeah. Lucky you.'

She ignored the sarcasm. 'By the by, that was a smashing
escape from Soho. Charles described it for me. We're all so
very proud of you, you know.'

Bolan was feeling more the heel with every passing
moment. Very solemnly, he asked the girl, 'What do you
people want from me, Ann?'

'Just now,' she told him, 'all we want is that you remain
alive. And we want you to allow us to help you accomplish
just that.'

Bolan could not argue a jungle logic into the situation. He
smiled faintly, a barely visible twisting of the lips, and said,
'Okay, we'll play it that way. For now. But keep one thing in
mind. As long as you are friendly to me, you have inherited
all my enemies – and those people play very rough games.
On the other hand, if you turn out to be *my* enemy ... well,
I have my rough moments also.'

45

'We understand all that,' she replied in a small voice. 'And we accept all risks.'

Bolan had no ready response, and they drove in silence for several minutes, heading back toward London via Cromwell Road. Then Ann told him, 'Gloucester Road is just ahead. Take a left there. We'll go up Paddington and cross to the north.'

'Where's our destination?' Bolan muttered.

'Queen's House,' she replied. 'You have the key in your pocket, I believe.'

'That's your place,' he said.

'Yes, it's my place. My *secret* place, count on that. It's safe there.'

'Okay, I'll count on it,' Bolan told her, staring stonily forward.

She leaned against him, resting her face on his arm. 'Don't seem so grim, Mr. Bolan. It will be just you and me. And we will . . . get to know one another far better.'

Bolan greeted the prospect with mixed emotions. A vision of the torture cells at *Museum de Sade* flashed through his mind. He glanced down upon the lovely head at his shoulder and experienced a trickling little tightness in his guts.

'Let's hope,' he murmured, 'that our familiarity does not breed contempt.'

'I have no worry about that,' she whispered.

But Bolan did. Which way, he wondered, was the tide running now?

CHAPTER SIX

CRISIS

BOLAN dropped off to scout the area on foot while Ann Franklin circled about to put the car away in a garage at the rear of the building. Russell Square turned out to be an attractive little park in London's northeast section, close by the University of London and the British Museum. Queen's House headed a row of neat Georgian town houses which angled away to the south of the square, in what appeared to be a neighborhood of family hotels, pleasant rooming houses, and old but probably expensive apartment buildings. Bolan's recon was thorough but swift, and revealed no evidence of enemy presence. He met Ann at the garage, picked up his bag, and they went into the house through the rear entrance.

To Bolan's surprise, the girl's apartment was very plain. Somehow he had expected a continuation of the erotic motif at *Museum de Sade*. Instead he found minimal furnishings, an almost masculine austerity of decor, and a library atmosphere.

'Welcome to Ann's Retreat,' the girl said quietly, then explained, 'I don't live here, actually. It's my run-away-to place when I feel the need of privacy.'

Bolan carried his bag on through the living-room and paused at the windows to peer through a crack in the draperies. It was still dark out, thin fog haloing the street lamps in the park directly opposite.

'Bedroom is to the left, kitchen to the right,' Ann announced. 'Which are you most interested in, bed or board?'

Bolan turned to her with a sigh and said, 'I'm suddenly running out of steam. Guess I'm pretty beat.'

'The loo is off the bedroom,' she told him.

'The what?'

She laughed. 'Sorry, the bath. You look as though you'd love to have one.'

'Thanks, I would.' He went into the bedroom and placed his bag on a chair and opened it. The girl was watching him – rather nervously, he thought – from the doorway. He removed his jacket and asked her, 'Okay if I put these things on some hangers?'

Her eyes were lingering on the gun harness at his chest. 'Yes, of course,' she replied in a near whisper. She pointed out the closet. 'Over there.'

The closet was totally bare except for a half-dozen wire hangers. Bolan put his jacket and his spare suit in there and said, 'Ann's Retreat, eh?'

'Yes,' she replied from the doorway. 'I told you that I don't live here. I live with Major Stone.'

'I see.'

She came on into the room then and stood tensely by as Bolan continued unpacking. 'I suppose I've given you a false impression,' she told him. 'Earlier, I mean. When I told you that we would . . . get to know each other. I did not mean . . . in bed.'

Bolan showed her a tired smile. 'Of course not,' he said.

'But it's nothing personally against you,' she hastened to add. 'Actually I . . . well it's simply . . . that . . . I-I'm terrified of men, you see. All men, not just you.'

Bolan stared at her through a moment of silence, then he nodded his head and said, 'Okay.'

He opened the false bottom of the suitcase and took out what remained of his 'war chest'. It had shrunk to a few thousand dollars, in bills of large denomination, and made a rather thin stack. He placed the money on the bedside table and lay the Beretta atop it, then came out of the harness and began removing his shirt.

Ann Franklin was fingering a nylon nightsuit he'd placed on the bed. 'You wear black underwear?' she asked solemnly.

Bolan chuckled. 'That's my combat uniform,' he told her. 'Some *soldados* I met in Miami told me that it strikes fear into the hearts of my enemy. But that's not why I wear it.

The color gives me a nighttime invisibility, and the skintight fit helps me in and out of tight places.'

'Like the commandos,' she commented.

'I guess so. That was before my time, though.'

She nodded. 'Mine also.' Their conversation was becoming less strained, more comradely. The girl had unfolded the suit and was holding it to her body. 'Does it keep you warm?'

'Pretty well,' Bolan replied. He was seated on the edge of the bed, removing shoes and socks. 'It's a thermal suit.'

'I see.'

'Did, uh, you really mean that . . . about men?'

She colored visibly and dropped the suit to the bed. 'Yes I — it's silly, I know. I suppose it's . . . the men I've known.'

'Like Major Stone, eh,' Bolan said quietly.

'Don't misunderstand that,' she quickly replied. 'Major Stone is the only father I've known. He's raised me from the age of 12.'

'Uh-huh.' Bolan pawed through the bag for his electric shaver.

She seemed to have a need to explain. 'Major Stone has never mistreated me, never. He's protected me from . . . all that. And he's always given me the best of everything.'

'Good for him,' Bolan murmured. He was suddenly very tired. 'I don't suppose you'd have any coffee around here.'

'Oh, yes,' she said, moving toward the doorway. 'You get your bath, and I'll be doing things in the kitchen.'

Bolan watched her out of sight, troubling thoughts nagging at him. None of this, he was thinking, made any sense at all. He was becoming too fatigued to care, however. He finished undressing and removed his watch, noting the time at close to seven o'clock. It had been a long night. It was cold in the bedroom, but Bolan was too tired to shiver. He picked up the Beretta and the shaving case and went into the bathroom.

Ten minutes later, Ann Franklin rapped lightly on the bathroom door and walked in. She carried a tray and was humming softly under her breath. Bolan was lying back in a tub of steaming water, seemingly utterly relaxed and half asleep in a sea of suds, but half-closed eyes were watching the girl's every movement.

She maneuvered a low stool alongside the tub and set the tray on it. Her eyes found the Beretta, jammed into a towel rack within Bolan's easy reach. Whimsically, she said, 'I've heard of *sleeping* with one's pistol, Mr. Bolan, but isn't this a bit ridiculous?' The comradely tone was gone, Bolan noted, replaced by the earlier tense nervousness.

'Survival,' he replied, his speech slurring a bit, 'is never ridiculous.'

Her eyes fell and she said, 'Of course you would know more about that than I. Well,' she added, with a forced perkiness, 'I have here coffee and muffins, which are also a matter of survival. Shall we break bread over the tub?'

Bolan grinned and reached for the coffee. She placed the cup in his hand and asked him, 'How long since you've slept?'

He carefully sipped the coffee, then replied, 'I forget.'

'Then it's been much too long.' She knelt on the floor beside the tub, broke a muffin, and held it to his lips. He ate, realizing that it had also been some time since that event. She told him, 'You are an unusual person, Mr. Bolan.'

'Not really,' he murmured. 'I'm an ordinary person in unusual circumstances. Are you still afraid of me?'

She hesitated, then whispered, 'As a person, no, I suppose not.'

'I'm afraid of you,' he told her.

Another pause, then: 'I don't find that particularly flattering.'

Bolan sighed. 'It's the survival instinct,' he explained, grinning tiredly. 'I have to suspect the very worst in everybody.'

'Then why survive?' she asked dully. 'I mean . . .'

After a brief and almost embarrassed silence, Bolan said, 'I know what you mean.' He had asked himself the same question, many times. Though Ann Franklin apparently could not, some thinker had long ago expressed her idea rather well: when love and trust are dead, then the man himself is dead and awaiting only official notification of the fact. Yeah, Bolan had considered the idea. And rejected it. He told the girl, 'I have a job to do. I live to do that job. That's what survival means to me.'

Small-voiced, she replied, 'You're speaking of your job as executioner.'

He sighed. 'Yes. That's the job.'

'You live only to kill.'

'That's about it.' He finished the coffee and returned the cup to her head.

'I simply cannot believe that,' she told him.

He shrugged. 'Then don't.'

'If you came to believe that I were your enemy, you would kill me?'

He smiled faintly. 'Are you my enemy?'

'No.'

He said, 'I've never killed a friend.'

She gazed at him with sad eyes, then got to her feet with a loud sigh. 'You have no *true* friends in England, Mr. Bolan. I suggest that you simply slaughter the entire population straightaway, and leave as quickly as possible.'

She went out, lightly closing the door behind her.

Well hell, Bolan told himself. She'd been trying to get him to open himself up, to give her something to admire, perhaps something to pity. For what? Games of conscience. She was mixed up in something she did not like, and she wanted someone to tell her it was all worthwhile.

Well, she would not get it from Bolan. He had a hard enough time keeping himself convinced. Right now, for example, it would be so easy to simply slip beneath the warm water and give it all up. No more fear, no more pain, no more blood, just blissful euphoria and quiet oblivion in the soothing warmth of Ann Franklin's bath. Why not? After all, who the hell was Mack Bolan to appoint himself physician to a sick society? So what if the Mafia cancer was spreading into vital tissues? – weren't there other surgeons around who were better equipped than Bolan for the job?

Wasn't it sheer ego that kept him on the job? They'd called him a Quixote in the press. They should have called him a cockalorum – yeah, that would be more like it – Sergeant Self-Importance, self-appointed Saviour of the Western World.

Bolan had gone for more than sixty hours without sleep. During that period he had been under constant stress, harassed by lawmen and the underworld alike while effecting a 'tactical retreat' covering hundreds of miles and many different modes of transport. He had fought his way out of four death traps and eluded the police of three nations, yet he had failed to make his way back to 'safe' territory. And now he was at the point of complete physical and mental exhaustion, his last bit of reserve strength fully gone, occupying a narrow ledge of questionable refuge in a world trying its best to swallow him.

Lesser men would have succumbed to the pull of defeat far sooner than this. For Bolan, the moment of defeat had come as a reaction to a young woman's visible disgust, and the wave that inundated him was the cresting of his own mind and soul in a deep pool of self-doubt.

For one infinite and timeless moment he hung there in suspension between the instinct for life and the comfort of death as he let go and slid beneath the actual waters of the warm bath – and then he came threshing out of it, coughing and spluttering and lunging for the Beretta.

Though his present danger was totally within himself, the depths of his exhaustion projected phantom enemies somewhere *out there*, and Dolan's response came from the very core of himself. When Ann Franklin stepped back through the doorway, in response to the commotion, Bolan was sitting upright in the tub. His fist was full of Beretta, suds were clustered about his face, his eyes were straining for focus, and he was muttering. 'It's okay, it's okay.'

The girl immediately understood the situation. She dropped to her knees at the tub, one arm going out to encircle his shoulders, the other hand gently and carefully working at the deathgrip on the pistol.

'Give me the gun, Mack,' she whispered.

'It's okay,' he told her.

Bolan was technically unconscious, and Ann Franklin knew it. 'Give me the gun,' she urged, 'before you get it all wet.' The struggle ended then. She took control of the Beretta and carefully placed it on the floor, then pulled the plug from the drain and put a towel about Bolan's shoulders. 'Let's go to bed,' she whispered.

He struggled out of the tub and steadied himself with a

hand against the wall while Ann towelled him dry, then she moved inside the arm and helped him into the bedroom.

'It's okay,' he told her again as she fought the covers back and guided his head to the pillow.

'Yes yes, I know,' she assured him.

'Where's my gun?'

She returned to the bathroom for the pistol, showed it to him, and shoved it under the pillow. 'How's that?' she whispered.

'Great.' Bolan's eyes focussed on the girl then, awareness flashed there, and he muttered, 'Hell, I'm naked.'

'Utterly,' she replied, smiling solemnly. 'Body and soul.' She flipped the covers over him and said, 'Get some sleep now.'

He was laboring to hold the focus. 'You asked ... why I bother to live. Okay. I live to win. When I die, *they've* won. Can't let them win, see. Show them ... they're not God. Throw death ... back in their teeth, see.'

'Yes, yes, I see.'

'That's all it means. Not ego ... not cockalorum ... it's tactics. That's the game. Beat them ... at their own game, see.'

'Yes. I understand that now.' She began removing her clothing, her eyes steady on his.

'What're you doing?' he asked thickly.

She removed her bra, waved it delicately over the bed, then dropped it to the floor. 'Getting ready for bed,' she replied. 'Girls sleep too, you know.'

Bolan lifted himself groggily to one elbow as she stepped out of the panties. 'Better not,' he growled. 'I'm not all that beat.'

'I wouldn't be so sure of that,' she replied solemnly. She slid in beneath the covers and snuggled over to him. 'I have a survival problem also, you know,' she confided in a quivery whisper.

He clasped her in both arms, pulling her in tight, and murmured, 'This is great.'

'Uh huh.' A moment later Ann felt his embrace slacken. Borderline consciousness had surrendered to complete exhaustion. She pushed him onto his back and adjusted the

53

pillow to his head, studied the strong face for a moment, then impulsively kissed his lips.

'Big bad Bolan,' she whispered, then nestled her face in his throat and very contentedly joined him in sleep.

For both of them, man and woman, a survival crisis had been reached and passed, each in their own way. It was not to be the final one for either of them.

CHAPTER SEVEN

COUNTERPOINT

THE Executioner's long night had ended, but across the
Atlantic, in an eastern U.S. city, that same night was just
beginning, with an informal meeting of Mafia bosses. The
site of the conference was the suburban home of Augie Marinello, head of a powerful New York family: the subject was
Mack Bolan, and what to do about him.

Contrary to popular myth, there was no 'boss of all the
bosses', or Chief Capo. There had been none since the violent demise in 1931 of the first and final *Capo di tutti Capi*,
Salvatore Maranzano. Instead, each Cosa Nostra 'family'
now had representation on *La Commissione*, or Council of
Bosses, which ruled the sprawling crime syndicate.

The present meeting was not a full council, but considerable power was represented there. In attendance were
Marinello and the bosses of two other New York families,
plus the overlords of several neighboring territories. Only
once since the embarrassingly aborted 1957 summit meeting
at Appalachia had a new full conference been attempted.
And that one, at Miami a short few weeks earlier, had
become a fiasco to wipe Appalachia out of the mind forever,
thanks to Mack The Bastard Bolan.

Now the eastern power clique sat in sullen thoughtfulness.
Each of the men present had been present also at Miami;
some bore visible wounds to remind them of the traumatic
event; all bore wounds of the soul which would never heal,
haunting their dreams and irritating their waking moments.
Miami would never be forgotten. Nor would the man who
had caused it all.

Two burly men in tailored suits moved silently about the
conference table, pouring wine from napkined magnums.

With this chore completed, they quietly withdrew and closed the doors on the convention of royalty.

Augie Marinello, host of the occasion, broke the silence with a deep-throated growl. 'So the bastard turns up in England,' he said.

Arnesto 'Arnie Farmer' Castiglione, chief of the lower Atlantic seaboard, shifted uncomfortably in his chair and explained, 'So I guess we didn't get him in France. I got to apologize for the bum dope. But I would've sworn . . . I mean, I just don't see how the bastard could have got out alive.'

'It looks like he did,' spoke up a Pennsylvania boss.

'Bet your ass he did,' said the man from Jersey. 'I got a bunch of dead soldiers over in England to prove it.'

Arnie Farmer grimaced. 'Don't tell me about dead soldiers. We're still counting the dead in France, and tryin' to get the rest out of jail.'

Marinello sighed loudly and sibilantly. 'I got word from Nick Trigger.' His glance flicked to the Jersey boss. 'He wants to take over the Bolan hunt.'

'I got a full crew over there right now, Augie,' the Jersey man advised.

'Sure, but how're they doing?' Marinello asked thoughtfully.

'Well . . . like I told you, they've made contact twice.'

'We made contacts all over the place down in Miami,' an upstate boss pointed out. 'So what's that make anything?'

'They're good boys,' Jersey argued. 'I think they're on top of it pretty good.'

'Bullshit,' said Arnie Farmer.

'Whattaya mean, bullshit?' Jersey flared back.

'I mean I sent a whole damn army to France, a regular AEF f'Christ's sake, and not even half of 'em got back. That's what I mean bullshit. I mean boys like Sammy Shiv and Fat Angelo and Quick Tony went to France and never came back, that's what I mean bullshit.' He tasted his wine, returning the angry glare from New Jersey over the rim of the glass. 'So who've you got in England that's on top of it pretty good?'

'I got Danno Giliamo and his boys,' Jersey replied through flattened lips.

Arnie Farmer raised his eyebrows in respectful receipt of this news and replied, 'Okay so I'm surprised you sent Danno. I take it back the bullshit remark.'

'Danno's a regular bulldog,' Marinello put in. 'Nobody'll say different to that – and listen – it's no dig at Danno that I'd like to see Nick Trigger take over the hit. Nick tells me that he talked this over with Danno – and Danno says it's okay with him. Listen, this is no time for hurt feelings. We've got to stop this boy, hard and fast. And the cost is getting out of hand, it's getting awful.'

'Not even mentioning the contract purse,' Pennsylvania added.

'I'd gladly pay twice,' Arnie Farmer Castiglione declared passionately. 'In fact . . .' He raised the wine glass to his lips and sipped delicately, then continued in a milder tone. 'I'm for upping the ante to a cool million. That'd make the scramble for real, and we already lost more than that on account of this boy. Besides that he's making us look foolish. How long are we going to stay in business if . . .'

The speech ended on the uncompleted question. Silence descended and reigned for a long moment, then the New Jersey boss grunted and suggested, 'Contract money is not the answer.'

'Then just what the hell is?' Arnie Farmer demanded, his voice rising with emotion. 'You can't cop a plea with this boy, you know.'

The latter statement had reference to an older and more painful period in the life of the boss from Jersey, who had served three successive prison sentences on 'copped pleas' – pleading guilty to a lesser crime to avoid prosecution of graver ones. He resented being reminded of these past indignities, and his angry face plainly showed it.

Marinello hurried into the breech. 'We already got the answer,' he declared softly. 'We are doing the right things, make no mistake about that. It's just a matter of—'

'No, wait a minute. Who says we can't cop a plea with this Bolan?'

All eyes turned to Joe Staccio, the upstate New Yorker. Someone growled, 'You nuts or something, Joe?'

'Maybe I am,' Staccio calmly replied. 'Then again, maybe

I'm not. I'm just saying it ain't all that far out an idea. Maybe we been acting like old-time hoods about this thing. You know? And even the old-time hoods found out there was more than one way of getting out of a problem. You know what I mean?'

Augie Marinello was giving Staccio a thoughtful gaze. Castiglione's lips had curled into a snarl as the full implications of Staccio's suggestion registered. The man from Jersey was watching Marinello.

Castiglione sneered, 'What do you want us to do, Joe? Throw up our hands and beg for mercy?'

'Now wait,' Marinello said, as the noise level began to raise in the conference room. 'Joe has brought up the question I'm sure all of us has thought about at one time or another. So now that it's in the open, let's talk about it. Maybe he's right and maybe we're going about this thing all wrong.'

'I was just thinking about the days of the old man,' Staccio quietly put in. He was referring to Salvatore Maranzano. 'Everybody was shooting at everybody else, nobody knew who to trust. I mean those wars got out of hand too, you know. If Charley Lucky hadn't made his peace, and forgave and forgot and patched things over, then none of us would be sitting here right now. Right?'

'You're right, Joe,' Marinello agreed.

Arnie Farmer drily observed, 'Charley Lucky Luciano and Mack the bastard Bolan are not exactly the same two people.'

'Yeah, you're right there, Arnie,' Staccio replied. 'But that's not the point, and it's not the right comparison. The point is, there's more than one way to end a war.'

'We're getting hurt,' the man from Jersey put in. 'And bad. Nobody is going to deny that. We've got to get this thing over with, one way or another.'

Marinello nodded and asked Staccio, 'Just exactly what was you thinking about, Joe?'

'A deal,' Staccio replied.

'What kind of a deal?'

'He forgives, we forgive. And we bury the hatchet.'

Arnie Farmer exploded with, 'What the hell has *he* got to forgive?'

58

'We gotta be realistic, Arnie,' the upstater explained. 'This boy lost his whole family, and he figures their blood is on our hands. Now if we understand anything at all then we just got to understand a debt of blood. Right? So I say let's agree that one debt cancels out the other. Let's be realistic and see if we can't end this damned war.'

Arnie Farmer fumed silently.

Marinello said, 'Okay, let's say that both sides agree to bury the hatchet. Then what?'

Staccio shrugged his shoulders. 'I haven't sat around and thought it out. But I think maybe Charley Lucky had the right idea, way back when.'

'You mean we invite Bolan into the organization,' Marinello said quietly.

Staccio again shrugged. 'Why not? It worked before, it could work again. He'd be a hell of a good boy on our side of the fence. We could all respect him, right? Wouldn't that boy make one hell of an enforcer?'

Arnie Farmer rose jerkily to his feet and delicately fingered the fabric of his trousers. 'I got a hole in my ass the size of a golf ball,' he announced in a voice thick with emotion. 'That bastard put it there, and I'll never sit down in peace again until—'

Staccio said coldly, 'You're not the only one. We all got our reasons for hating that boy's guts. But that's not the point. We got to be realistic. Our whole thing is going to fall apart around us if we don't start using our heads instead of our hots. Now we got a crisis, just like with the old wars. We got a crisis and we got to face up to that!'

Castiglione shivered. 'Cop a plea with Bolan,' he muttered, '. . . never! I mean *never*!'

'Hey, hey, let's cool it off,' Marinello suggested. 'You've both made your point, now let's sit down and discuss it, eh.'

Castiglione sat, but growled, 'You try burying the hatchet with this Bolan, you're gonna tear our thing apart for sure. There's too many scars, Augie, entirely too much to try forgiving and forgetting.'

'Okay, okay, let's just talk about it,' Marinello urged.

The Pennsylvania boss said, 'What if we just made Bolan *think* we wanted to deal? Huh?'

59

'Don't you think he'd be smelling for that sort of thing anyway?' Staccio replied. 'He's going to be suspicious as hell. I doubt if we could get him to listen even if we were a hundred percent sincere.'

'So we're just wasting our time anyhow,' Arnie Farmer commented. 'Why are we wasting our time talking dumb ideas?'

'I got a boy,' Pennsylvania said quietly. 'He could get to Bolan.'

'You mean Leo Pussy,' Marinello replied thoughtfully.

'That's the boy. Sergio's nephew. He's running my Pittsfield action now. I think he—'

Staccio interrupted with, 'That's the boy was with Bolan back when?'

'Yeah. I guess he could make the pitch if anyone could.'

'What pitch?' Castiglione cried. 'We ain't decided on no pitch!'

'I mean,' Pennsylvania explained, 'if we decide to go that way.'

'Save us all a lot of time: I'm not deciding that way!'

Marinello said, 'No harm in talking it over, huh Arnie? Let's think of it as flexibility, huh? Maybe we could have *two* things going at once. Like Appaloosas and stevedores . . . you catch?' He winked again, while shielding his face from the view of Joe Staccio. 'Like a horse race, eh?'

'I don't know what you're getting at,' Arnie Farmer Castiglione said sullenly.

'Well, let's just talk the possibility. Suppose we set up two programs. Huh? We turn Joe loose at this end, turn you loose at yours, see who gets to the finish line first. Huh?'

'Bullshit,' Arnie Farmer replied.

'No, I'm serious.' Marinello's glance flashed to the Pennsylvania boss. 'You really think this Leo Pussy could get next to Bolan?'

The other shrugged his shoulders. 'If anybody can, he can.'

The shrewd eyes moved to Staccio. 'How about it, Joe? You want to sit down with Leo the Pussy and discuss things?'

The upstate man nodded solemnly. 'I'll give it a try.'

'I say bullshit,' Castiglione coldly commented. 'I already tried that route. Trying to get next to Bolan, I mean. I sent him a nigger friend. He sent me back a planeload of dead soldiers.'

'I still think it's worth a try,' Staccio insisted.

'All right, let's talk it up this way,' Marinello suggested. 'Arnie, you head up the contract campaign. You'll have Nick Trigger as your number one boy, and you sure can't complain about that. You also got Danno and his crew. You add whatever else you think you need, and you go after Bolan's ass. Joe, you take whatever you need and go after his *head*. How about it? Does it make sense? I'm asking all of you, now. What do you think?'

'I still say bullshit,' said Arnie Farmer. 'But I'll go along with it, even if it is dumb . . . if that's what everyone wants. But understand this. I take no responsibility for what happens to Joe or this Leo the Pussy. We'll just get in each other's way, and my boys are going to be shooting first and talking afterwards.'

'Why do you keep saying it's dumb?' Staccio asked.

'Because,' Castiglione replied, 'if this Leo can get next to Bolan, he can get there also with a gun in his hand . . . and I don't see—'

'What you don't see is that Bolan is more than a common rodman. That boy has a sixth sense about this stuff. I been studying him, ever since Miami. I keep thinking about the Talifero brothers. Also I just can't forget this fantastic stuff he pulled off at Palm Springs, against Deej and his boys. He's got something going for him, I don't know what. But you got to remember, every cop in the world is after this boy's ass, just like us. And he keeps dancing away from them just like he does us. It's a sixth sense, that's what, and he can smell a trap two days before he gets to it. He's—'

The boss from New Jersey interrupted with quiet laughter. 'Maybe he uses black magic, Joe,' he said. 'He puts on this black suit and turns into a devil or something.'

Another man at that table shivered and said, 'Shit, don't even kid about that.'

'What I'm saying,' Staccio went on grimly, 'is that I have to go into this thing with a very sincere approach. No tricks, no traps, straight all the way. The horse race ends the minute I make contact. We got to get that straight right now. And whatever I make with Bolan, I make with all the authority of the full council. It's got to be like a contract hit – all the families have got to honor it. That means everybody, not just us here now, but all of us, and that means Arnie the Farmer Castiglione and the Virginia blue-bloods.'

Marinello had been watching Castiglione during the speech. He nodded, his eyes still on the man from Virginia, and said, 'Our word is our honor, Joe, like always.'

'Okay, just so we all understand that. Otherwise, if I got doubts myself, then Bolan will tumble to it, and then Joe Staccio is in one bad spot.'

Castiglione smiled wryly and observed, 'I believe Joe is superstitious.'

'No, he's right,' Marinello said. 'I go along with that, Joe. If we can come to an agreement here, between us, then we'll set up a telephone conference with the others and we'll get it all ironed out. So what do we say. Are we agreed to try it?'

'We gotta know the terms and the details, Augie,' Pennsylvania said.

'Well we got all night to knock it around, huh?' Marinello replied.

'Let's talk my end first,' Castiglione suggested. 'I'm already thinned out over Bolan. I'd like to have a crew from each family, and that means they pay their own way, too.'

'I'll loan you Jimmy Potatoes and his crew,' Pennsylvania shot back.

'I'll send Tommy Thompson and company,' said Marinello.

'Scooter Rizzo,' chimed in another New York boss.

'Okay, that's great,' Castiglione said. 'When you set up that phone council, I'll want talent from each of them, too.'

Marinello solemnly nodded his head. 'Okay. This is a great approach. Now let's talk about the other end. How do you figure we can support your effort, Joe?'

'Well, first of all, let's talk about the package I'm going to offer Bolan. It's got to be attractive. I mean, not just a truce, but something he'd really go for, something with a future.

Let's talk about rank in the organization. With the Talifero boys temporarily out of the picture, we need a hard arm for the *Commissione*. I'm thinking—'

'Aw shit!' Castiglione cried, aghast with what Joe Staccio was thinking.

'No now, wait a minute, Arnie,' Marinello said, favoring his old buddy with a sly wink. 'Let's let Joe talk about it. Go ahead, Joe, I believe we're getting somewhere.'

'Okay,' Staccio said, 'what I'm thinking is . . .'

And so it went, into the long night at Mafiaville, with frayed nerves, heated passions, cold fears, and a stab at reality. The final result of this 'crisis conference' would find a terrifying impact on Mack Bolan's violent domain, and the severest test yet of his holy war with the underworld. Bolan's long night had not ended. It had only just begun.

CHAPTER EIGHT

PSYCHED IN

BOLAN awoke to total darkness. His hand found the grip of the Beretta and he lay very still until his mind had found its place and he knew where he was. With this knowledge came a wavering image of a beautiful girl with flawless flesh snuggling to him in a warm embrace, and he had to wonder if the memory was valid. He was alone in the bed now, that much was certain; he pushed silently away and reconned the darkness until satisfied that no other presence shared the apartment with him.

He returned to the bedroom and turned on a lamp. His digital calchron revealed that fourteen hours had elapsed since his arrival at Queen's House, and the clutching at his stomach was indicating that he'd been much too long without food. The flat's heating system was functioning now; he had no sensation of discomfort as he padded nakedly about the bedroom for his clothing. He donned the black nylon nightsuit and strapped on his gunleather, then went straight to the kitchen. Eggs, milk, and bacon were in the refrigerator. He immediately stirred two raw eggs into a glass of milk and consigned this to his clamoring stomach, then lit the fire under the coffee pot and returned to the bedroom.

It was then that he found the note from Ann Franklin. It lay across his stack of money and read, 'Meet me at Soho Psych at 11:00 P.M.' Lying atop the note was a glossy book of paper matches, the embossed cover proclaiming that Soho Psych was the swingingest place in London. It also provided the address of the meeting place.

Bolan finished dressing, adding herringbone tweed slacks and jacket and a fresh shirt and tie over the skinsuit. He pondered briefly over the money, then transferred most of it to the little pouch at the waist of the nightsuit. The only small bills, two american fifties and five British 10-pound notes, went into his wallet.

By 9.30 he had consumed a comfortable mass of bacon and fried eggs, and the quart of milk, and was topping off with lukewarm coffee. It was time to move out. He went quietly down the rear stairs to the garage, opened the trunk of the Lincoln, and contemplated his arsenal. The *Uzi* submachinegun went under the front seat, along with a stack of ammo clips. It was a fine little weapon, using the standard N.A.T.O. round and featuring a folding stock which reduced overall length to about seventeen inches. After a brief mental debate, Bolan took the Weatherby and a belt of ammo to the apartment and stashed it in the bedroom closet. Then he returned to the car and drove to the edge of the Soho district, found a parking place on a side street around the corner from *Ronnie Scott's*, the renowned jazz club, and joined the foot traffic on Frith Street.

Here was London night life in all its late twentieth century splendor ... and squalor. It was Greenwich Village and Fisherman's Wharf rolled into composite, an assortment of joints, dives, stripperies, fish-and-chip houses, fine restaurants of all nations, and the ever-present discotheques and go-go palaces. Bolan strolled casually through the neon jungle, orienting himself and getting the feel of the area, walking in an atmosphere of far-out jazz, electronic flashers, and the jarring crescendos of rock amplitudes. He found Soho Psych precisely where the matchbook advertising promised he would, 'on Frith, just off the square', snuggled in between a Pakistani restaurant and a rundown theatre whose billboards offered 'the best in London flesh'.

Bolan was an hour early, and this was by design. He went on by the club, crossed the street at the corner, and wandered back slowly. Diagonally across from his target was a budget self-serve restaurant, calling itself a tea house but very obviously a cafeteria. It provided tables near the front windows, and though Bolan's appetite had been fully sated in Ann Franklin's kitchen, he entered and went through the motions of purchasing a meal, filling his tray with an assortment of selections from the buffet.

The girl at the cash register glanced at his tray and said, 'That'll be six and six, sir.'

Bolan was reaching for his wallet. He said, 'Six and six what?'

She smiled understandingly and inquired, 'American?'

Bolan nodded and slipped a ten-pound note from the wallet.

Still smiling, the cashier explained, 'Your bill is six shillings and six pence, sir.' Then she saw the ten pound note, the smile faded, and she asked, 'Is that the best you can do?'

He muttered, 'I'm afraid so.'

The girl made change for his seventy-eight cent purchase from an equivalent twenty-four dollar note, gave it to him rather grumpily, and watched disapprovingly as he casually dropped the change to the tray and made his way to a front table.

He dawdled there for forty minutes, forcing himself to eat some of the steak and kidney pudding, grilled tomatoes, and several other tidbits of English diet. His view of the street was unobstructed, and he was cataloging all traffic in and out of Soho Psych.

At ten minutes before eleven a cab stopped at the club and Ann Franklin emerged. Bolan lit a cigarette and watched as she leaned back in to say something to another passenger, a man, who was obviously staying with the cab. Then the vehicle went on and the girl entered the club. Bolan waited and watched. Another cab came up minutes later – perhaps the same one, Bolan surmised – and a man got out. Bolan recognized him as the big one who had chauffeured them from Dover – Harry Parks, the girl had called him.

In the corner of his vision, Bolan became aware of another vehicle quietly edging to the curb some yards behind the cab. It was a smallish car of English make. Two men debarked and threaded their way casually along the sidewalk, then entered Soho Psych a few steps behind Harry Parks. The car moved forward and another man stepped out just above the club, and crossed over to Bolan's side of the street. Bolan watched this last man, studying him intently, as the man lit a cigarette and leaned back against a lamp pole as though waiting for someone.

Bolan knew who the man was waiting for. He sighed and unbuttoned his shirt, withdrew the Beretta and held it in his lap as he affixed a silencer to the barrel, then returned the pistol to the side leather. The stage was fully set, it seemed, awaiting only the appearance of the principal.

So the principal left his observation post and went outside.

Bolan stood at the curb, gazing up and down the street for any further obvious signs of the hardset awaiting him. There were none, but the man at the lamp pole immediately stiffened to attention and flipped away his cigarette. Somewhere along that street, Bolan knew, another outside man had been waiting for that cigarette to fly. Bolan casually stood his ground and waited. Evidence came quickly from the direction of Soho Square, as another man hurried across the street and took up a position on Bolan's other flank.

Bolan smiled grimly to himself and crossed over to the club. He was not overly appreciative of intrigue; the time had come to make the cut between friend and enemy, to determine precisely where Ann Franklin and the Sades stood in that separation, and to engage the enemy – whoever they might be – in open combat. As he entered the club, the two men behind him started across the street.

An immaculately dressed older man stood just inside the door at a foyer desk. A quiet sign announced that only members were allowed on the premises. Bolan went immediately to the desk and told the man, 'I'm meeting a young woman here. Maybe you—'

The doorman interrupted. 'You'll still be required to purchase a membership, sir. It's the bloody law 'ereabouts. It take three quid, sir, plus another ten bob entry fee.'

Bolan dug for his wallet and asked, 'How much is that in pounds and ounces?'

The man chuckled 'Bloody confusing for you Americans, I know sir. Never mind, we're shifting to the decimal system ourselves by and by. Then we'll all be bloody well confused.'

The two men had come in from the street and were hovering near the door, trying their best to look disinterested in the proceedings at the desk.

Bolan fingered the bills in his wallet and asked, 'How much?'

The doorman was looking at something on a note pad. He said, 'Would that be Miss Franklin you're meeting, sir?'

'That's the one.'

'Then I'll beg your pardon, your entry is all piped up. Sorry sir, I just took the carpet at eleven, and I 'adn't time to read me notes.'

'Does that mean I go on in?' Bolan asked.

'Oh yes sir, to be sure sir. You proceed on through the bar, down the stairs, across the clubroom, and up again to the mezzanine. Room number three, sir.'

Bolan dropped a tenner on the desk and said, 'Let's keep our little secret.'

The ten-pound note disappeared immediately beneath the doorman's hand. He said, 'We're the soul of discretion, sir. By the by, are those two gentlemen at the door accompanying you?'

Bolan said, 'Not hardly.'

'I'd say that's a bit unfortunate then, sir. Those chaps are Scotland Yard.'

Bolan's eyebrows rose. He murmured, 'Thanks,' and went on into the spider's den.

The game had changed, disconcertingly so, but there was no turning back now. The only way out led straight into the jungle.

CHAPTER NINE

TRAP PLAY

SOHO PSYCH was fairly representative of the rock music clubs that proliferate upon the London scene, most of them appearing and disappearing with amazing rapidity. This one was unique chiefly because of its seeming permanence. It had remained on the 'in' list for several seasons, drawing locals and tourists alike and packing the house nightly while competitors rose and fell in cycles typical of the new mod culture of swinging Londontown. The club had become a favorite watering hole for local musicians as well as visiting ones, and thus was also a favorite of the 'groupies' – the young girls who followed the rock groups about.

The bar itself offered no live entertainment, unless the nude models who posed in glass cases, tall tubes, really, all about the place could be classed as entertainment. The bar was overflowing with a standing room crowd and the conversational level was about equivalent to roaring surf on a rocky shore. The only light came from the glass tubes of the living mannequins, in varying and changing shades, each girl changing her pose with each alteration of the lights. No one seemed to be paying much attention to them.

Bolan paused in front of a statuesque blonde mannequin to light a cigarette, wondering why the two cops had not moved on him out there in the lobby. Perhaps, Bolan surmised, they were under orders to attempt no immediate apprehension – perhaps Bolan had popped up before they'd had time to get set the way they wanted to be. So now they would be getting set, and with jaws of steel.

He lingered at the girl's tube, waiting to see if the two would come in from the lobby. As a matter of idle curiosity he tried to catch the mannequin's eye but she seemed totally oblivious of his near presence. Then her light changed from red to a deep purple and she shifted from a demure wood-nymph pose to one of ecstatic abandon – head thrown back, one knee raised and angled across the other leg, hips thrust forward. Bolan grinned and went on. London could be an interesting town, he was thinking, to a guy who had plenty of time for playing. Not so for Bolan; Scotland Yard had just invaded the bar.

Bolan found the stairway and descended to the major arena. It was a large room with a seemingly endless sea of close-packed humanity, deafening amplifications of wild music, and a bewildering display of psychedelic lights. On a center bandstand a large rock combo seemed to be in a noise competition with a singing group who were screaming into separate mikes at the limit of their physical systems.

He pushed through the riotous confusion and reached a stairway at the opposite side, then paused to gaze back along his route of travel. The two 'chaps' were on the other stair-way, anxiously perusing the crowd below them. Bolan went on up to the luxuriously carpeted mezzanine and along a narrow hallway to a private dining-room with the numeral three on the door.

It was hardly more than a cubicle, darkly intimate in candlelight, with a small round table for two positioned at a draped window overlooking the clubroom. A low couch oc-cupied one wall; a couple of small harem pillows completed the picture. The room was also partially soundproofed, the noise from below only faintly audible.

Ann Franklin sat at the table, a glass of water clenched tightly in both hands. She had been peering through a crack in the draperies, watching the scene downstairs. Her head snapped toward the door as Bolan entered. Something on his face froze her smile as it was forming. It wavered and col-lapsed and her gaze went quickly back to the window.

The man called Harry Parks pushed himself up from the couch and exclaimed, 'You're late! We was beginning to wonder if—'

Bolan snapped, 'Cops followed you here. At least four of them are in the club right now.'

Parks gave his head a concerned shake and replied, 'Yes, I

70

was just telling Annie I thought someone was on our tail. We was 'oping you wouldn't be coming in. Thank the lord they didn't spot you.'

'They spotted me, all right,' Bolan corrected him. 'And they could have easily moved on me, but they didn't. The question is ... why not? They're setting something up. I guess I'd like to know what and why.'

The big man took a step toward the door. 'I just guess I'll be finding that out,' he declared.

'Quietly,' Bolan commanded.

'I know me business,' Parks muttered, and went out.

Bolan dropped into the chair across the table from Ann Franklin. Their legs collided. The girl hastily withdrew hers, threw Bolan an embarrassed glance, and hastily lowered her eyes.

He told her, 'Thanks for warming my bed.'

Softly she replied, 'You're quite welcome.'

'Thanks for a lot of things,' he added solemnly.

The gravity of the situation overcame the girl's embarrassment. Her hand shot out to rest on his and she hissed, 'You must get away from here. You are in very great peril.'

Bolan said, 'Hell, I know it. But you set this up. Now what's it all about?'

'Major Stone requested the meeting. He should have been along before now, and I'm quite worried that he isn't.'

Bolan, also, was 'quite worried'. He asked her, 'Why meet here? Why not at the museum?'

'For many reasons,' she replied. 'None of which are worth discussing now. Just please go.'

'Uh-uh. Not until I get the story.'

'What story?'

'I find myself in the middle of some very messy intrigue. I don't like it, Ann. So you tell me now, quick and straight, what's it all about?'

'I'm sorry,' she said quietly. Obviously it was all she intended to say.

'Okay and bye bye,' he said, just as quietly.

He was up and moving when the girl cried, 'Wait!' and ran after him, catching him at the door.

71

Bolan took her in his arms and folded her into a bruising kiss. The movement took her by surprise and for an instant she resisted, then she melted into the embrace and gave herself entirely to the moment of passionate delirium. When he released her, she moaned and held onto him, pressing in for more.

Gruffly he demanded, 'Tell me about the Sades. Why all the interest in Mack Bolan?'

She was breathing raggedly, still in the grip of the tensions engendered in that tight clutch. 'I don't know it all,' she gasped.

'Then give me what you do know.'

She disentangled herself and leaned against the door, struggling to regain her composure. 'Mack, I-I'm sorry for acting like a . . . a . . .'

'Forget that,' he growled. 'Come on, you owe me some answers, and my time is running out.'

The girl took a deep breath and said, 'The American Mafia has moved into London. I suppose you're aware of that. They are trying to take over everything here, as I hear it. It's a big power play, involving politics and industry and just very nearly everything. And they were not being too successful.'

'Until what?'

Her eyes skittered away. 'Until somehow they got onto Major Stone's club. Somehow they came into possession of . . . of some highly damaging and politically explosive, uh, items of evidence.'

Bolan sighed. 'Okay, I could have guessed,' he commented quietly. 'I take it that some of the members of your club are Very Important People.'

She nodded. 'And they are now in a terrible squeeze.'

'That bad, eh?'

'Yes. You've heard of the Profumo scandals, back in the sixties?'

Bolan said, 'Who hasn't?'

'Yes, well – this could be ten times worse. These gangsters have information that could rock the government – perhaps topple it.'

'Is the Major directly involved in this?' Bolan inquired.

'Not directly, no. But he feels responsible. It was *his* security that was breached.'

Bolan said, 'Tell him I'll be thinking about it.'

She murmured, 'It's like a terrible nightmare, all of it.'

He glared at her for a brief moment, then smiled suddenly and said, 'Don't take it so hard, we'll figure something out.' His hand found the doorknob. 'Where will I find the Major?'

She shook her head. 'I can't imagine, nor can I imagine what has delayed him. If you can get out of here, return straightaway to Queen's House. We'll try to contact you there.'

Bolan's smile broadened. 'Come to think of it, we do have some unfinished business there, you and I.'

She managed to keep her gaze steady, and whispered, 'Yes, so we have.'

He patted her arm, cracked the door for a quick look, then slipped outside and pulled the door shut behind him.

Harry Parks moved up quickly from the stairway and hissed, 'You were right, mate. It's getting to be a beehive down there.'

Bolan pointed to another stairwell at the far end of the mezzanine. 'Where does that go?' he inquired.

'Rooms, next floor up,' Parks replied, then added, '*Bed* rooms, for them that can't wait.'

'And above that?'

The man shrugged. 'I never felt a need to know. Do you mean to go out that way?'

Bolan said, 'I mean to try.'

'Then I guess I'd best be going the other way, and raisin' a fuss.'

'I'd appreciate that,' Bolan told him.

The big man grinned and said, 'It's me speciality,' and went quickly back along the passageway toward the main clubroom.

Bolan hastened to the other end of the mezzanine and found that the stairway he'd spotted also went down to a lower level. As he paused to ponder this revelation. Major Stone appeared below him, hurrying up to the mezzanine.

Each became aware of the other at the same instant.

73

Bolan's Beretta leapt into his hand; the Major halted abruptly and glared at him and his face took on a vexed expression. 'Out through the front, Bolan,' he commanded. 'You've not a moment to lose.'

Bolan replied, 'Can't. The joint's alive with cops.'

Stone moved on cautiously to the head of the stairs, his brows knit with thought. 'Then I've gotten you into a pretty pickle,' he announced. 'I have been darting about for 20 minutes in an attempt to shake Nicholas Woods off my tail. I finally ditched my car several streets over and made it in through the back way. But I've no assurance that I lost them, not entirely.'

Bolan asked him, 'And who is Nicholas Woods?'

'A local mobster, and I'm surprised that you don't know. I believe he is also referred to as Nick Trigger.'

Bolan said, 'Okay, I make. Now tell me, how many of them?'

The Major shrugged. 'At least five, perhaps more. I suspect they're prowling the alleyway at this very instant.'

Bolan sighed, his mind racing ahead to his options. He could try bluffing his way out past the cops, and if they closed on him he would have no recourse. Bolan did not shoot cops. To reverse the Major's trail would undoubtedly run him into a direct confrontation with a superior force of gunners.

He told Stone, 'Okay, I'm going over the top. Ann's waiting for you in room three.' Then he charged on up the steps to the floor above.

A hardfaced little man occupied a wicker chair at the top of the stairway. His eyes quickly discovered the gun in Bolan's hand and he cried, ' 'ere now, what's this?'

In a rough imitation of Harry Parks' speech, Bolan told him, 'It's a pinch down below, mate. Get 'em all out, quickly now!'

The man's hand jerked to a button on the wall behind him, and Bolan could hear alarm bells sounding immediately in the rooms along the hallway. The little man was on his feet and intent on scurrying down the stairs, but Bolan restrained him. 'Not that way,' he growled, hoping for a different exit.

74

'There ain't no other way,' the man screeched. He tore loose from Bolan's grasp and bounded down the stairs.

Already pandemonium was erupting into the hallway as men and women in varying stages of nudity spilled out of the rooms. An angry youth hobbled past Bolan, trying to get into his trousers on the run, a shirt clenched between his teeth, shoes beneath his arms. A pretty girl hurried along in the youth's wake, fumbling with the buttons of her dress and trying to cover nakedly heaving breasts while she hurled taunting insults ahead at the boy.

Bolan felt like hell about it all, but he knew the interrupted lovers would live this problem down; perhaps Bolan would not. He watched the unhappy group stream by, then he began a quick inspection of that upper area of Soho Psych. It consisted of six rooms, three to each side, and apparently covered only the rear section of the building. The rooms to the front had windowless, blank walls – it appeared that the upper story of the building was subdivided, with a separate mode of access to that part which faced on the street. The other three rooms each featured a small window over the alleyway. Bolan's recon consumed less than a minute and revealed that he was in a seemingly hopeless situation. There was no sign of a fire escape, no way to the roof, and nothing but a sheer drop to the alley some thirty feet below.

He was about to give it up as a bad stand when he found the way out. In the ceiling above a closet in the end bedroom was a trapdoor access to the attic. He hoisted himself up and through and carefully replaced the covering, then used his cigarette lighter to orient himself in the darkness. As he had hoped, the attic was common to the entire building and yawned out in front of him with no apparent obstacles. It was rough and without flooring above the ceiling beams, and with a low overhead – very low in spots, giving evidence of a gabled roof layout. This suited Bolan fine; gables meant an uneven roof surface, sometimes attic windows, and very possibly a way out.

He extinguished the lighter and began a careful exploration, crawling across the ceiling beams and seeking a light source. Here and there a rat scrambled across his path, setting Bolan's teeth on edge. Sounds of a wild commotion on the floor below were drifting up to him when he spotted his light source – a faint rectangle of dim light far ahead. He pushed on with greater haste, knowing that every second counted now.

The light was coming through a latticed ventilation window, set into a vertical section of roof just a few feet above the ceiling beams. The lattice was composed of wood strips which were brittle with age, and the opening was just wide enough to pass Bolan's shoulders.

The strips gave easily to his gentle pressure, breaking with a dull snap as one by one he quickly cleared the opening. A brief head-through recon showed a short drop to a flat section of roof just below but very narrow – and Frith Street angling off way below.

Bolan reversed his position and went out feet first, clinging to the rotted wood of the window frame for support. Something was going on down in the street in front of the club, but Bolan's line of vision did not afford him a view of that particular area. His interest was not especially strong in that direction anyway, and he was carefully working his way around the gable and toward the rear.

He then discovered that the roof was common to the entire row of buildings. It was an uneven and jumbled surface, however, and steeply sloping in spots, but some moments later he had made his way along to the far end and found a place to go over the side – an iron ladder set into the ancient bricks at the rear – and he descended quickly to the alleyway, alighting just a few yards from the junction of alley with street.

No sooner had he dropped to the ground than a rough voice exclaimed, 'Hey what the hell!' and a large figure leapt out of the shadows of the building a few feet downrange. The voice was American and the revolver that swept into view was definitely antagonistic.

Bolan's sideways dive was an uninterrupted extension of his drop from the ladder, and he was slapping leather in the same movement. He hit the ground and the trigger of the Beretta at the same instant, the powerful little weapon phutted softly through the silencer, and the shadowy figure jerked about and crumpled against the building with a quiet gurgling sound.

A man in a long overcoat appeared immediately at the mouth of the alley and called out, 'Johnny? What's going on down there?'

The Beretta whispered again, and the man in the overcoat probably never knew what was going on down there. He fell forward into the alley, a pistol clattering along in advance of the sprawl, and Bolan passed the remains at full gallop, erupting into the side street with Beretta swinging and ready.

At that same moment car lights flashed into brilliance, from the curb just downrange. Bolan saw the spurts of muzzle fire streaking out from behind the lights even before the thundering reports reached his ears, but he was already across the blinding glare and arching down toward the vehicle, his own quiet replies sizzling into the argument and dead on target.

A cacophony of police whisles were sounding up on Frith Street and the sounds of excited activity were swirling around the corner and along the side street. A loud British voice of authority bawled, 'This is the police! Cease your fire immediately!'

Bolan's fire had already ceased, as he was beyond the seal car and disappearing into the darkness, but someone in the vehicle was turning his fire toward the police. A volley of answering fire swept down the street and sieved the heavy car, and quiet abruptly descended as Bolan faded around the far corner.

He was clear, for the moment, and he had thrown death back into their teeth once again. But how much longer could it go on? How many more trap plays could he blitz his way out of, and how much longer could he remain clear of these wily men from Scotland Yard?

The London War was taking on a decidedly personal hue, and the Executioner was getting angry. He could not continue on in this purely defensive mode of combat. If he was to survive, he knew, he was going to have to take the offensive. His soul protested, but the battle-hardened flesh

77

knew the truth. Full scale warfare, *his kind* of warfare, was the only route to survival in England.

And he knew where he had to start. He reached the Lincoln, transferred the *Uzi* from the floorboards to the seat, and set off for the *Museum de Sade*.

The Battle for Britain was on.

CHAPTER TEN

THE CELL

BOLAN was in combat uniform: midnight skinsuit, black sneakers, the little *Uzi* dangling from a neck strap, Beretta harnessed to his side. He was making his final approach on foot. The night was quiet, cold, and smotheringly black; Bolan was hardly more than a moving extension of the darkness, a silent shadow gliding across the London nightscape. He had stripped off his outer clothing and left the car inconspicuously parked, several streets back.

He entered the square from the side opposite the museum and paused there. It was dark, all dark. He waited, taking a patient audio recon. Several minutes later his patience paid off. He heard sounds of human presence: a shoe scraping cement somewhere in the blackness ahead, a brief and muffled sound of voices, a subdued cough.

The enemy was here. This time they were showing real respect for the man they hoped would show up. They had done something to the street lamps; all were extinguished, as though the London blackouts had returned. Only the most diligent listening could disclose any sounds. At the museum, across the way, a faint suggestion of light showed on the ground floor. Bolan remembered the heavy draperies at all the windows, and guessed that the museum might not be as deserted as it seemed.

He went on, more slowly now, stepping with extreme care and staying close to the line of buildings. Someone sniffled, just ahead. Bolan halted. A foot scraped, and Bolan saw a barely discernible movement in the blackness, hardly more than a hint of bulk outlined in the stygian background. When, he wondered, would they ever learn to use dark clothing on a nighttime stakeout? He moved forward again, barely breathing, until he was close enough to reach out and touch the man, who was leaning against the building, his hands in the pockets of his overcoat, his snapbrim hat pulled low over his forehead.

Bolan knew how difficult it was to remain alert and ready during these long quiet waits in the night. With all sense perceptions deprived of stimuli, often a mild form of vertigo resulted. Some men would literally go to sleep on their feet. This one was obviously in some lethargic state: he sniffed halfheartedly, trying to clear his nostrils of a troublesome mucus, and turned his head to look directly at Bolan.

The blackclad figure sprang forward then, in one swift movement pinning the man's head to the building and clamping a hand over the mouth, the other hand striking simultaneously in a stunning chop to the throat, his knee following through with a paralyzing smash to the dia-phragm. The sentry stiffened in a momentary spasm, an in-voluntary squawk of pain and alarm dying unexpressed in the clamped-off mouth, and then he became a soft mass flowing toward the ground. Bolan helped him down in a quiet descent and quickly checked for a sign of continued breathing. There was none. The respiratory system was totally overcome by the shock of the attack. The wild black cat moved on through the jungle of night to the next target and repeated the process, with identical results. Then he re-versed his ground and went to the other side of the square, seeking a man with a cough. He found him, and quietly cured the cough. Next stop was the porno bookshop and the entrance off the alleyway.

He had taken note of the store's lock on his previous visits. It was an ancient mechanism of dubious value. The blade of a knife applied at the proper spot, and then the insistent pressure of a shoulder, silently overcame the resistance. Bolan went inside.

He went down through the basement and along the pass-ageway, coming up in Edwin Charles' security cellar be-neath the museum. On his first time through, Bolan had paid only passing attention to this area of the building. He had simply wanted to get out, and he had very little curiosity regarding the location and operation of the security monitors. Now they were a prime consideration.

The night before, Charles had led him from the ground level down the stairs and along a rather narrow cellar passageway to the manhole of the tunnel. Bolan had noted the two heavy doors at each side of that passageway and had assumed, without further interest, that the old man conducted his spying from behind those doors. Now, both stood slightly ajar. This time Bolan went exploring. Behind one door, he found himself in a spacious and elaborately furnished basement apartment. It was a single room affair but apparently held every conceivable convenience, including even a wet bar with tap beer and a handsomely outfitted electronics workshop.

No one, however, was at home.

Behind the door on the opposite side of the basement Bolan found the 'security station'. It was far more elaborate than he had expected. An impressive electronics console and a battery of closed-circuit television monitors dominated the scene. Various other gadgets, including a film editing table and a projector, were present. Edwin Charles was not.

First to draw Bolan's interest were TV monitors. All were activated, and the conglomerate seemed to be providing a complete surveillance of the first two levels of the building. One screen showed the entry hall, another a wide-angle shot of the clubroom in which Bolan had found himself imprisoned the previous night, still another the erotically decorated harem room – in several camera angles – and each of the small cells on the upper level had its own monitor.

Those cells had been feebly lighted and deserted during Bolan's earlier visit. Now they were lit well enough to allow televised surveillance, and none of them were deserted. Young men and women appeared to languish there in attitudes of suffering and submission, all naked and cowed and bound into the various types of imprisoning devices.

The monitors showing the harem room were something else. Here men and women lay about in a variety of luxurious accommodations, and in a scene combining the best of *Arabian Nights* and the wildest in *Roman Orgy*. A party was most emphatically in progress, and just as emphatically it was geared to the most offbeat varieties of erotic delight. Most of the men, it seemed, were middle-aged or beyond – except for an occasional consortium of aged lechery with pretty lad. The women were without exception young and beautiful, and there were many. Everywhere Roman togas mixed and contrasted with colorful harem pajamas, slave girl costumes, and the inevitable devices of 'bondage'.

On a small revolving stage at the center of all this, a huge black man was spread-eagled upon a simple upright cross, bound hand and foot. He was nude, and he was obviously in a state of wild sexual agitation. A tall blonde girl, also nude, was tantalizing him with a lewdly suggestive dance in which she frequently wriggled against him then swayed back to avoid his wild lunging after her. Following each of these sallies, the big fellow was punished for his impertinence by another girl, an Amazonian figure, with a wicked looking black whip. It was theatre in the round, *à la Sade*, and it made Bolan's guts creak. He had to wonder how many other acts had preceded this one across that small stage, and he began to understand what Ann Franklin had meant by 'a paid staff'. These people were performers, *actors* and damned convincing ones in their own peculiar speciality. Even the cell-sufferers were undoubtedly acting out a role with all the stage vigor of any thespian anywhere. TV monitors were banked about the revolving stage, allowing the audience to also keep track of the activities in the cells.

The console in the security station apparently was geared more to the entertainment angle than to items of security. Bolan wondered if they had video-taping capability – and he also wondered if the revellers upstairs realized that they themselves were on candid camera. Talk about blackmail mills – this one was a natural goldmine for anyone with such ambitions.

His attention was drawn to the monitor showing the cell with a barrel balancing trick. An Amazonian beauty in weird garb had just stalked into camera range in that cell. She wore thigh-high boots of glossy black leather and a tightly laced corset affair that sucked her into an hourglass from armpits to hips. Cutouts at the chest provided a free and high projection of magnificently sculpted breasts. Thick black hair descended in a free fall to her waist. Grotesque facial cosmetics conveyed a convincing impression of satanic evil. She must have stood six feet tall even without the high-heeled boots, Bolan guessed, and she carried the inevitable black whip.

A well formed young man occupied the balancing platform. His back was to the camera; he was imprisoned by the wrist irons with his face to the wall. The devil girl went directly to the task at hand, lashing out energetically against his nude flanks with the whip. He reacted with a believable display of pain, lunging away from the stinging tips of the lash, losing his footing, clawing desperately at the chains to relieve the harsh pressure at his wrists – just about as Bolan had visualized the thing earlier.

The performance was too realistic for Bolan. He supposed that the whip was made of some sort of trick material, but it was still too much for his stomach. He whirled away from the console, wondering what had become of Charles and what had prompted the old man to desert his station and leave it wide open. This was obviously a party night at the museum, certainly no time for the security watch to be relaxed.

Bolan made another quick inspection of the entire basement area, returning none the wiser some minutes later to the control room. During his absence the black man had left the stage in the party room and another act had replaced him. This consisted of two young men lashed nakedly together back to back and two girls bound to each other in a side-by-side arrangement. The nude foursome's problem of the night was an erotically obvious one, and their frantic attempts at resolving it were acrobatically ingenious.

Bolan's attention was suddenly diverted from the Siamese-twin act by a peculiar movement across the screen of one of the cell monitors. A satanic Amazon had uncharacteristically staggered past the camera lens, her face showing genuine shock and revulsion as she hurried out of the little room. Bolan bent closer to the monitor. The scene there, at first look, seemed a typical one. A 'victim' was imprisoned in a variation of the stocks – a particularly evil device consisting of a small platform raised a few inches above the floor, in which were set ankle holes for imprisoning the victim's feet; just behind this was another platform slightly higher off the floor, with holes for neck and wrists.

Bolan had noticed the contrivance on his trip through the maze, and there had been no puzzle as to its function. The victim would be required to bend over double, standing in the stocks in a grotesque position with his head practically between his feet. Too much bodily fatigue, vertigo, dizziness, or any other circumstance which would cause the victim to sway too much in any direction would undoubtedly choke him. Total imbalance would result in a broken neck. Bolan had gathered all this in one quick glance, the previous night. Now he realized that he had not grasped the full diabolicalness of this device. In its present usage the victim was doubled over *backwards*, and an extra feature had been added. A narrow platform, resembling a sawhorse with steel spikes along its back, was thrust under the arched spine. If this had been a staged act, the role would have called for a contortionist.

But this victim was no contortionist. The closer inspection sent chills along Bolan's spine and sucked all the moisture from his mouth. This victim was no performer. He was quite an old man, and there was simply no way to feign the racking distress of that distorted body. The camera angle was in bad relation to the lighting, besides which only the back of the victim's head showed – but Bolan knew immediately what had become of Edwin Charles.

An animal growl rumbled past Bolan's lips and he was out of there and running up the stairs to the ground level before his thinking mind took charge. He erupted into the small room which lay just beyond the clubroom and smashed through into the party chamber. The scowling black-clad figure with submachine gun in hand went virtually unnoticed through the crowd. Indeed, he looked no more out of place there than anyone present, and he received his first challenge at the labial doorway.

Two of the leather-clad Amazons guarded that portal, standing stiffly spread-legged with crossed arms and dangling whips. The satanic-pretty faces registered puzzlement at Bolan's aggressive approach. At the last moment, one of the girls expertly curled her lash about Bolan's chest and the other stepped into his path. The whip, he found, was of soft and harmless nylon. The girl herself was something else, as big and strong as she seemed.

Bolan snarled, 'The old man's in trouble!' and pushed the girl roughly aside. He went on through and up the stairway, with one of the girls right at his heels and panting along in hot pursuit.

He had only a vague idea as to his destination as he hurried through the cellular maze, but he knew he was getting warm when he spotted a devil girl crumpled to the floor in a doorway.

To the girl following him, Bolan snapped, 'Help her!'

He stepped over the unconscious girl and into a reality much more horrible than could be gathered by a TV camera. The unmistakable smell of blood was mixed with the acrid odor of burnt flesh to overpower the atmosphere of the tiny airless cell; death had come there to release human agony and misery, and Bolan knew it the moment he stepped through that door.

Here was one old soldier who had not merely faded away. Edwin Charles had died hard.

The sawhorse affair was built of adjustable wooden legs and an iron crosspiece with conical protrusions along its top. The iron section had recently been intensely hot, and still was radiating considerable warmth. A blow torch lay discarded on the floor in the corner of the cell. Bolan decided that this had been used to heat the iron of the medieval device, which was then positioned beneath the arched back of the old man and probably slowly raised in height until the brittle old spine could no longer accept the demands placed upon it. He had sank back onto the red hot iron, and it had literally eaten its way into him.

It seemed likely also that the spine had snapped, and perhaps other bones as well. The red heat of the iron bar had probably cauterized and sealed ruptured blood vessels as it advanced into the body, but bleeding of an internal nature had found its natural exit through both the bowel and the mouth of the victim. It was a macabre scene. Bolan could understand why even the devil girl had fainted.

He grimly inspected the remains and muttered, 'The things men do to one another.' Then he stood there for a moment in angry contemplation of a grand old soldier's final moments. What was it the old fellow had said about the museum? Something about a deeper meaning, a sign of the times.

Bolan grunted, 'Yeah,' and went back out. He found the two devil girls leaning weakly against each other in the next cell.

'Is he dead?' whispered the girl who had chased Bolan up the stairs.

'He sure is,' Bolan muttered. 'Just how long has this party been going on?'

'Since eleven,' the girl replied in a funereal whisper.

Bolan looked at his watch. The time was then shortly past midnight. He shook his head and said, 'I don't know how long the old man has been in that room, but he hadn't been dead for more than half an hour.'

The implications of that decision hit him immediately. Edwin Charles had died with his agony on full display in the party room below, the reality of the gruesome scene concealed by the bogus suffering going on all about him. Quietly, Bolan told the girls, 'He's been dying through half of this nutty party.'

The girl who had fainted seemed in danger of doing so again. Her hands clutched at Bolan for support and she told him, 'I was in and out of there many times. I didn't know he was . . .' Her eyes rolled. 'Until it started to *smell* so terrible . . .' She looked as though she wanted to be sick.

'Who puts these people into these nutty devices?' Bolan asked.

The other girl murmured, 'Normally they attach themselves, and they can get out any time they wish, without aid. It's all in fun, you know. I mean, who would've thought . . .?' Her naked breasts shuddered with the unspoken horror of the idea and she swayed toward Bolan.

He steadied her and muttered, 'Yeah, this is some kind of fun place,' and then he left them to console one another and he went back through the harem room. Little had changed down there, except that the frantic foursome had discovered a way for *sex en masse* to overcome the physical limitations of human anatomy.

The cell of Charles' final agony was in prominent display just above this living exhibition. As he walked past, Bolan drew his Beretta and sent a quiet round into the monitor. There would be no more ghoulish jollies from an old man's final torment.

He passed on through, spurned the stairway to the basement, and strode purposefully toward the main exit. As he approached the door, he loaded the *Uzi* and made it ready. Mack Bolan was in killer mode, and his mood was now definitely inclined toward thunder and lightning.

CHAPTER ELEVEN

THE PRISONER

DANNO GILIAMO sat in quiet thought on the rear seat of a large black sedan which was parked just off the square near *Museum de Sade*. He was alone except for one other man who sat quietly huddled over the steering wheel. The sound of an approaching vehicle intruded into the silence. Moving slowly, it swung close then halted at the curb just opposite Giliamo's car. A man stepped out and the car moved on. A moment later the sedan door across from Giliamo opened and Nick Trigger slid in, hastily closing the door to deactivate the domelight mechanism.

By way of greeting, Giliamo emitted a bored sigh and said, 'I guess you was right, Nick. He ain't showed up here. Nothing on your end either, huh?'

'Nothing, hell,' Trigger replied quietly. 'We had plenty on my end. But you were right about that lucky bastard, he's as slippery as melted jello.'

'You mean he got away again?' Giliamo replied in a dulled voice.

'Yeah, he got away.'

'Well he ain't turned up here.' Giliamo nervously tamped a cigarette against his fist then shoved it between his lips and lit it, his eyes weary and disturbed in the glow of the lighter. 'So what happened?' he asked.

Trigger sniffed and settled deeper into the seat. 'We had him bottled in a rock joint over by Soho Square.' The massive shoulders raised and settled again in a tired shrug. 'He busted out, that's all, got away clean. And cops all over the God damned place, I mean crawling out of every hole.'

Giliamo took a nervous pull at the cigarette and asked, 'Okay, so what happened to my boys?'

'Six of your freelancers are dead,' Trigger reported with a sigh. 'Also Looney and Rocky got arrested. Don't worry, I'll have 'em sprung first thing in the morning.'

Giliamo mouthed a string of half-audible obscenities, then said, 'You see what I been up against, Nick?'

'Yeah.' The London enforcer punched his elbows into the backrest with a loud sigh. 'I don't see any sense in hanging around this neighborhood, Danno. Leave a couple of boys to keep an eye out, just to make sure, but I guess we might as well tuck it in for the night. Bolan isn't going to run from one setup right to another. Arnie Farmer and his army is due in first thing in the morning. We'll huddle with them and see what we can come up with.'

'I was hoping to get it all over with before they showed up,' Giliamo muttered. 'Do you know this Arnie Farmer?'

'We met a couple of times,' Nick Trigger replied heavily. 'Do I get it right that you feel about this *capo* the way I feel about him?'

'If you mean is he an uncomfortable so and so to be around, then we feel the same way, Nick, yeah you got it right.'

'Then you might as well come out and say it. Arnie Farmer is a bastard, and I don't like him coming over here. I wish he'd stayed home.'

'That's exactly right,' the Jerseyite muttered. 'And I wish to God we could've got Bolan before the other bastard showed up.' His eyes flicked to the man in the driver's seat. 'Nobody better not go repeating that, though. Right, Gio?'

Gio Scaldicci, the wheelman, swivelled about with a grin. 'Right, Mr. Giliamo. I got ears that don't hear nothin' that's not spoken to 'em.'

The two men in back settled into an uncomfortable silence, then Nick Trigger said, 'Well, I'll ride back with you, Danno. Let's get out of here.'

'We gotta wait, I got Sal out on the street makin' his rounds. He'll be back in a minute.'

The three *Mafiosi* sat through a protracted silence, then a front door opened and a fourth man hastily entered the car. This was Sal Masseri, one of Danno's crew leaders. In a choked voice, he announced, 'We got three dead soldiers out there, Danno.'

'What do you mean?' the New Jersey *caporegime* growled.

'I mean Willie Ears and Jack the Builder and Big Angelo are dead as hell, that's what I mean. No blood or nothing, they're just laying there dead. I think their necks are broke or something.'

Giliamo was speechless. He gaped at his companion in the rear, then made a lunge for the door. Nick Trigger quietly restrained him and asked Masseri, 'How long have those boys been dead, Sal?'

'I'd say no more'n ten or fifteen minutes. I went on around and warned the other boys. Nobody's seen nothing, though, Nick, not a damn thing.'

'Ten or fifteen minutes,' Trigger repeated musingly. 'That means he could have hotted it straight over here and . . .'

Giliamo slid forward to the edge of the seat and craned his head for a tense inspection of the hulking outline of the museum, just around the square from their position. In an angered tone, he declared, 'That cuts it! That bastard has found some way to get in and out of there without being seen. I'll bet he's in there right now.' He tapped his driver on the shoulder and commanded, 'Pull around there slow and quiet, Gio. Park in front of that bus stop.'

The car moved quietly around the corner and eased to the designated spot, directly across the street from the museum.

'Are we going back in there?' Masseri asked nervously.

'Bet your ass we are,' Giliamo barked. 'You get out there and pass the word along.'

Before Masseri could react, two men ran quietly up to the vehicle. Giliamo lowered his window and thrust his head outside. One of the new arrivals breathlessly reported, 'We just wanted to tell Sal that we found something. Over there.' He pointed to the opposite side of the square. 'A book store. The back door has been jimmied open. It could mean something.'

'Awright, take some boys and check it out,' Giliamo commanded.

The men jogged away. Masseri said, 'Maybe I ought go see what they got, Danno.'

Nick Trigger chuckled coldly. 'I think Sal is awful anxious to stay out of my little playhouse,' he observed.

'As a matter of fact he is,' Giliamo answered for his man. 'And that goes for me double, but that don't cut any ice. You stick right here, Sal. We'll give Stevie a chance to check out that store, and then we're gonna be moving.'

'Well, I don't like it either,' Trigger growled, 'but I guess not for the same reasons. There'll be too many people in there now. That means too many witnesses. Besides that, we're messing up the sweetest little operation I ever walked into.'

Gio Scaldicci turned toward the rear seat and asked, 'How'd you ever get onto a creepy joint like that, Mr. Trigger?'

The London enforcer shrugged his shoulders. 'You learn to use what's available, kid, and don't forget that. Don't ever forget that. That creepy joint as you call it has given our thing a clean sweep in this part of the world. I just hate to see it getting messed up, that's all. Especially over a crumb like this Bolan.'

The four men sat in a strained silence for another long moment, all eyes glued to the building across the street. Presently a man approached from the other side on a dead run. He pulled up panting beside the vehicle and reported, 'Stevie's found a tunnel! He wants to know should he go on through!'

'O' course he should go on through!' Giliamo snarled. 'Tell 'im to goddammit be careful and remember who he's going against!'

The messenger sped back into the night.

Giliamo said, 'Well, well.'

Nick Trigger produced a revolver and swung out the cylinder to check the load. He sighed and clicked it into place and said, 'I guess we better go in just the same, Danno.'

Sal Masseri swung outside with a Thompson sub under one arm, then leaned back in for a word to his boss. 'I'll bring the other boys over, Danno,' he said tightly.

'Do that.'

'Uh, listen Danno. Big Angelo was a good boy. Anybody can have any part of Bolan they want, but when we get 'im, I get the target practice on his nuts.'

'Sure Sal, I know how you feel,' Giliamo told him.

Masseri walked off into the darkness, the Thompson cradled casually in his arms.

Nick Trigger opened his door and slid his feet to the ground, remaining seated in the open doorway, no longer concerned about the dome light. He said, 'I've got a feeling.'

'Me too,' Giliamo replied. He opened his door and stepped onto the street, then paused to glare across the roof of the car toward the museum. 'He's in there, I know it.'

At that precise instant a door opened across the way, dull light spilled forth, and a solitary figure in black stalked out. He halted and framed himself momentarily in the lighted doorway, then he sent a burst of fire from an automatic weapon into the air, and immediately disappeared into the surrounding darkness in a diving leap. The Executioner was no longer 'in there'.

The driver of the Mafia vehicle gasped, 'Well, dig that cool bastard!'

But he was talking to himself. Danno Giliamo had gone to ground behind the car and Nick Trigger was scrambling for cover inside. The automatic weapon chattered again, but not harmlessly into the air this time. The window glass of the big vehicle exploded in an inward shower and Gio Scaldicci's head underwent an explosion of its own, pieces of the skull flying into the rear seat amid bloodied bubbles of brain tissue, and what was left of Gio slumped forward onto the steering wheel. The horn began sounding in an endless wail and presided over the louder booms and staccatos of combat weapons as thunder and lightning enveloped the night outside *Museum de Sade*.

It had not been an act of mindless bravado that sent Mack Bolan through that lighted doorway. He was angry, yes, and disgusted right down to the shivering center of himself, but the combat specialist had known precisely what he was doing.

The idea was *blitz*, from the German word meaning *lightning war*, and the intent was to shock the enemy, disorganize them, perhaps demoralize them, and then destroy them. Bolan knew what he was doing, from the first harmless burst into the air to all that followed.

The lighted car directly opposite his position had been a godsend. Even though he had just come from a lighted environment and his night vision had not been given time to develop, he was of course aware of the men grouped in and about that lit vehicle, and it was a natural target. The second burst from the *Uzi* went in for maximum effect. He saw Gio Scaldicci's head fragment, he saw the big guy in the rear scrambling for the floorboards, and he saw Danno Giliamo rolling frantically across the square in search of darkness. But heavy fire was already coming back at him from various areas of that darkness, and Bolan wanted to see more.

His third burst was to reach the gas tank and to make fractional sparks ignite the ready fuel into a bonfire. He was rewarded: the big car went up in a towering fireball and with an explosion that rocked the earth beneath his feet.

But since someone out there had a Thompson, Bolan was not standing still for the thundering sweeps of that big chopper. He moved out with the shock of the explosion, circling deep around the fire and trying to get behind the main force, in the hope of backdropping them against the roaring flames. Someone rose up right in his path, grunting with surprise and fear, and Bolan cut him down with the butt of the *Uzi* without breaking stride. He was following the traffic circle now, running along the street and coming around in the general area of the bookshop, moving recklessly through the open. Darkness was nowhere in that square now, the yellow glare of flames licking about in a wavering illumination of the entire area. The whole enemy force was apparently converging on the burning auto, shooting at only God knew what, Bolan didn't, and shouting excited instructions back and forth in a pyramiding scene of confusion.

Bolan reached the position he sought and threw himself to the ground at the curb of the traffic circle. The horizon thus presented was a beautiful one, to a combat infantryman, with the enemy highlighted as well-defined shadows against a blazing background. He emptied three clips into those shadows, grouping carefully and conserving the flow of ammo through the chattering weapon, until suddenly there was nothing left to shoot at.

Bolan lay there for a moment, listening and looking and refueling the *Uzi*. Utter silence had descended, except for the whooshing of the flames of the burning car. Bolan arose, inviting fire but receiving none, then slowly advanced across the island inside the traffic circle. The dead and the dying were sprawled about, and the hated smell of blood was everywhere he walked.

Too easy, Bolan was thinking, *much too easy*.

He stepped around a groaning man and found the man with the Thompson submachine gun lying on his back directly opposite the flaming vehicle. The guy was alive, but not very, though he was conscious and still gripping the Thompson to his chest. Bolan kicked the heavy gun away and said, 'What's your name?'

'Get fucked,' the guy whispered, and coughed up a hemorrhage.

'Who did it to the old man inside?' Bolan asked.

'Get . . . fucked.'

Bolan moved on, peering at faces, trying to spot Danno Giliamo. The burning car was still roaring furiously. The firefight had been incredibly brief. Only now was the first reaction coming from the people inside the museum. Bolan was aware of blinds being whisked back and of faces peering out from the ground level windows.

And then he became aware of something far more menacing. Through the open door of the museum had erupted three men, all armed, one of them carrying a shotgun. Bolan's *Uzi* was instinctively up and ready but he hesitated, unsure of the identity of the three. They were gaping about at the scene of incredible carnage with disbelief projecting all the way out to Bolan.

The frozen confrontation held for a split second that seemed much longer, then the man with the shotgun gasped, 'It's Bolan!' and made a fatal move. The *Uzi* chattered at the same instant that the shotgun boomed; the man fell back into the entrance hall, zipped from groin to gullet, and

Bolan's burst became a blazing figure-eight that swept the other two off the porch. Nothing heavy reached Bolan, but hot little things had dug at his ribs at the moment of the big boom, and he knew that he had picked up some pellets.

He wheeled about and went quickly back the way he'd come. He had just about pushed his luck too far, and it was time to be moving on. The police would be showing up any minute, and there was a familiar warm stickiness under his arm. He crossed the square, went past the bookshop, and on some subconscious impulse paused at the entrance to the alleyway and was swinging the *Uzi* about when something moved back there in the darkness and a choked voice urged, 'Hey shit, don't, I'm outta bullets.'

Bolan had already dodged back to the corner of the building for cover. He growled, 'Send the gun out first, then yourself, hands on head.'

A pistol hit the cobblestones and slid into view, then a thickset man moved hesitantly out of the shadows and into the flickering light of the square.

Bolan jabbed the muzzle of the *Uzi* into the man's belly. The guy sucked in his breath and said, 'Hey shit, it's hot. The barrel's hot, huh?'

Bolan withdrew the little chattergun and spun the man around, shook him down for weapons, then pushed him forward. 'Start walking,' he commanded. 'Straight ahead.'

'Where we going?'

'Depends,' Bolan said. 'Who are you?'

'I'm Stevie Carbon. I'm in Danno's crew, under Sal Masseri. Or I *was*.'

'Are you all done living, Stevie?' Bolan asked in a conversational tone.

'No sir, I sure hope not,' came the strained reply.

They moved swiftly to the corner. Bolan shoved the man down the street toward the Lincoln. 'Okay, Stevie, just keep on walking. Nice and quick and don't look back.'

'Where we going?' the man wanted to know.

'Maybe to hell.' Bolan allowed the neckstrap to support the *Uzi* while he probed his ribs with careful fingertips.

'Christ, can you tear things up in a hurry,' the man declared, striving for a buddy-buddy tone. 'I figure I got no arguments with a guy like you. I mean, nothing personal you know.'

Bolan knew a surge of weariness – not of the flesh but of the soul. 'That's the screwy part of this whole thing, Stevie,' he said coldly. 'There's nothing personal in any of it, is there? And then we run into an old man who's been tortured clear out of his body. And suddenly it gets very, very, personal.'

The man stumbled, caught himself, and quickly raised his hands again to clutch the back of his head. 'Uh, tell me straight out, Bolan. Are you gonna kill me or not?'

'That depends, Stevie.'

'On what?'

'On what you can tell me.'

'Look I don't know nothing, Bolan. Besides that, uh, I've taken the oath of silence. You know about that, huh.'

'You can die with that oath then, Stevie, if that's the way you want it.'

'You know I want to *live* with it, Bolan. You know that.'

They walked on in silence, Bolan two paces behind his prisoner. Police sounds rose up in the distance, and Bolan felt like this was where he'd come in. They reached the Lincoln. Tiredly, Bolan commanded, 'You drive.'

'Where to?'

'Like I said, Stevie, maybe clear to hell.'

They got into the car and the man said, 'I'll talk to you, Bolan.'

'Start the car, then you can start your mouth,' Bolan told him.

Though he was cold as ice on the outside, Bolan was experiencing an inner glow which meant that things were definitely beginning to look up. He had himself a prisoner of war, and not just an ordinary POW, either.

Bolan had no idea who Stevie Carbon was, or had been . . . but he knew who he was not. He was not the man seated next to him.

The Executioner had grabbed off a *caporegime*.

His POW was none other than Danno Giliamo.

CHAPTER TWELVE

THE INTERROGATION

NICK TRIGGER, in all his years of gunbearing for the brotherhood, had never suffered such personal humiliation. He felt defeated, disgraced, and deeply dismayed at his own cowardly reaction to imminent death. He was alive, though. He kept telling himself that he was still alive, and that surely this counted for something. There was no profit for the family in a dead hero. When a guy saw how things were going, when he saw that nothing he could possibly do would change anything – then surely staying alive was more important than dying. Death was such a final damn thing – it never really seemed possible that a guy could actually cease to exist, not until he came face to face with death. Then he knew, yeah shit, boy, he really knew.

And what could he have done against that Bolan at a time like that? An act of God, that's what, had spared him from cremation in that damn car. He shivered violently in the mere remembrance of it. Another second, just one more second if he'd stayed with that car, and there'd be nothing left of Nick Trigger right now but a little pile of ashes. If he hadn't had sense enough to get the hell out of there when he did ...

Nick was rationalizing his actions, and he was conveniently forgetting the fact that sheer revulsion, not combat sense, had driven him out of that car. Gio Scaldicci's blood and brains were all over the back seat and floor, and Nick had found himself lying face down in the mess. He had flung himself on through and out, and he'd been no more than ten feet away when the explosion came. Then he lay there stunned and half unconscious while Bolan chopped up Danno's hunting party. He had lain there also and watched the bastard in black walking quietly among the dead. He had heard him try to question Sal Masseri, and still Nick had lain there, his gun no more than a couple of feet away from his outstretched hand, and he'd played dead, and he had even said a couple of prayers.

He hadn't moved a muscle until after Bolan had struck down Stevie Carbon and the two boys he'd taken through the tunnel with him. Then, as Bolan walked back across the square, Nick slithered away in the other direction. He hadn't gotten to his feet until he was completely clear of the square, and then he'd jumped up and started running ... *running*!

He was appalled at himself, despite the rationalizations. Nick was beginning to understand, though, why Mack Bolan had remained so long alive against everything the brotherhood had thrown at him. He understood why Danno had seemed so awed of the guy, so willing to humble himself and ask for help from someone outside his own family. When that Bolan bastard made a hit, he didn't fool around with no light feints. He didn't just hit, he broke hell all around a guy. For Christ's sake, who wouldn't lose his head at a time like that?

Well, something had to be done about him. Some thing that hadn't been tried before maybe, some new wrinkle. They couldn't let that guy get away with that kind of shit. Until a few minutes ago, Bolan had been just a name to Nick, something to hit, just another name on a contract and another job and maybe another rung up the ladder of rank. That was all changed now. He had seen at first hand what Bolan could do.

Nick himself had brought death to more than a hundred men, yet it had remained for a guy like Mack Bolan to introduce Death to Nick Trigger, to make it a personal experience that Nick Trigger could understand. He understood it now, all right, and he wanted more than anything else to share that understanding with Mack the Bastard Bolan. He would, too, he decided.

The luckiest part of the whole fiasco, for Nick, was that nobody else knew. Apparently only Nick had survived. Nobody would ever have to know that Nick Trigger had played dead and watched the bastard turn his back and walk away, nobody would have to know that Nick had even been there when it happened.

Yeah, that was the luckiest part of all. Or so Nick Trigger thought.

They were rolling slowly up Tottenham toward Regents Park, and the conversation was accomplishing very little in the way of intelligence. Giliamo was glibly avoiding direct answers to sensitive questions, playing his role of dumb street soldier to the very hilt. Bolan had decided to let him play . . . for a while. They swung onto Marylebone and up to Park Road.

'Go in the park,' Bolan directed.

'Into the park, Bolan?'

'That's what I said, Stevie.'

They crossed over the tip of a lake moments later and Giliamo nervously asked, 'What're we doing here?'

'That depends,' Bolan told him. 'There's an open air theatre straight ahead. I want you to stop there, Stevie.'

The blood at Bolan's ribs had congealed, the wounds minimal, the pellets from the shotgun blast obviously having grazed the ribs and gone on. Still, there was some discomfort there and Bolan was finding his patience beginning to fray.

They pulled to a halt in the theatre circle. Bolan said, 'Give me the keys and get out.'

Giliamo did so, watching his captor narrowly as Bolan slid out from the other side.

'Over there,' Bolan said, waggling the *Uzi*.

'Over where?'

'Up on the stage.'

Giliamo stared at Bolan for a silent moment, then whirled about and trudged away with Bolan close behind. They climbed the steps to the stage, then Giliamo blurted, 'Hey look, what the hell are we doing up here?'

'You like to act, Danno,' Bolan quietly replied. 'I thought I'd give you a stage.'

The big man stiffened, then sagged noticeably. His voice was muffled with anger as he said, 'If you knew who I was, why'd you let me keep it up?'

'Get out there at the center of the stage,' Bolan commanded.

'You go to hell,' Giliamo snarled. 'If you're gonna kill me, do it right here.'

Bolan rapped him across the face with the butt of the *Uzi*, not lightly. Giliamo staggered back, holding one hand to the injured jaw, and went where Bolan directed.

'Down on your knees,' Bolan said.

The *caporegime* glared at him, but did as he was told.

'Where do you want it?' Bolan asked, thrusting the *Uzi* forward.

Giliamo choked on the words. 'You know I don't want it anywheres, Bolan.'

'You've been bullshitting me for ten full minutes, Danno. You can stop it now anytime you want. You can stop something else too, Danno.'

'You know I can't. If I talk, and you don't kill me, then they'll just do it later on anyway. I'd rather just get it over with right here.'

'Who's going to know you talked, Danno? Who's going to tell them?'

The Jerseyite was thinking about it. Presently, in an almost inaudible voice, he asked, 'Just what is it you want to know?'

'Who did it to the old man?'

'You ast me that a dozen times already! And I still don't know what you're talkin' about!'

'The old man in the museum, Danno. Who tied him up like a turkey and shoved a hot iron under his back?'

'Shit, I don't know what you're talking about, Bolan, that's God's truth.'

'Are you saying that you or none of your boys did it?'

'That's what I'm saying, whatever it is.'

'You were in that museum, Danno.'

'Sure. I was in there for about a minute. Me'n Nick, and Sal, and one other boy I can't think of his name right now. But we didn't do nothing to no old man.'

'Who is Nick?'

'Nick trigger, also known as Nick Endante. Maybe you

heard of him. He used to work for *Don* Manzacatti, way back when.'

Bolan was becoming more and more satisfied with the tone of the interrogation. Giliamo was loosening up nicely. He said, 'Yeah. So what is Nick Trigger doing in England?'

'He's enforcing.'

'So what was he enforcing at that museum tonight?'

'Nick was my contact here, see. I come over about a week ago, while you was in France. Look, I didn't ask for the lousy job, Bolan. I never wanted it. I got nothing personal against you. But when the bosses say go, the Danno Giliamo goes. You gotta understand that.'

'Yeah, I understand that, Danno. But about this Nick Trigger. How'd he get onto that thing at the museum?'

The prisoner was obviously working towards a decision, a very important one to him. Life and death hung in the balance, and his soul was sweating. He grimaced and said, 'You're putting me on one hell of a spot, you know that.'

Bolan shrugged his shoulders. 'It's just between you and me, Danno. But you better make up your mind. I'm not standing out here all night.'

'How do I know you're not going to execute me anyway?'

Bolan shrugged again. 'I guess that's just the chance you have to take, Danno. But for what it's worth, I don't kill my friends. Not even temporary ones.'

Giliamo took a deep breath and said, 'Okay. What was it you ast me?'

'I want to know the connection between Nick Trigger and that museum back there.'

'Well, like I said, he's enforcing. He's got some hooks into the guys that run that place. I don't know what exactly. They're a bunch of queers or something I think, and Nick's got it into them over that I guess.'

'Okay, so how did he know to look for me there?'

'Honest to God, Bolan, I don't know. Nick isn't – *wasn't*, I guess he's a toasted weenie right now – he wasn't the most talkative boy around. He called me up the other night and told me to look for you at Dover. He even gave me the name of the boat and the time and everything. Then after we lost you down there, he told me to look for you at that joint, that museum up there. That's all I know about it.'

'But you guess he had a pipeline, eh?'

'Yeah, it sure looks like it.'

'Okay, now about tonight. You said you were inside the museum. When was that?'

'That was about ten thirty, maybe a quarter 'til eleven. But we didn't see no old man. There was just this uppity little prick, talked with a fancy English accent. We spent most of our time just getting up there where he was at, hadda tramp through all those queer rooms. They got some sick stuff in that joint, Bolan. Or I guess you know about that.'

Bolan said, 'Yeah.' His jaw had stiffened and his mouth was suddenly quite dry. 'What about those little rooms on the second floor? What was in them?'

'Buncha fuckin' torture stuff, you know what.'

'No people?'

'No people 'cept us. What're you getting at?'

'This little guy,' Bolan said. 'About five-six or seven? Stiff as a ramrod?'

'Yeah, that's the guy. Talked to us like we were dirt, and him queer as a three dollar bill I guess. I felt like sluggin 'im.'

'What'd you talk to him about?'

'Not me, it was Nick. They went off to themselves and parleyed about something. Just took a minute, then we left. Nick—'

'Who else did you see in there, besides this little guy?'

'There was a lotta people down in that cunt room, you know, kids. Getting ready for a party or something, I guess.'

'Okay, go on with what you were saying about Nick.'

'What was that?'

'You left. Then Nick did something.'

'Oh. Well, Nick sat out in the car with us 'til this guy came out, about ten minutes later. Then they took off together.'

'*Who* took off together?'

'Nick and this queer little prick. They took off together.

Few minutes later the other queers started draggin' in. In fancy limousines, some of 'em. Cars dropped 'em off and went on. I never went back inside after that.'

Thoughtfully, Bolan said, 'But there were three boys inside during the firefight. They came out and threw down on me.'

'Well, that was something else all over again. Those boys found a tunnel or something, just before the fight started. We figured that was your way in and out, and we found your callin' cards – the three boys with the broken necks or whatever. Those boys went in under the ground to smoke you out, Bolan. That's all I know about that.'

'I think you're giving it to me straight, Danno,' Bolan said quietly.

'I am.'

'Okay, just one more thing. Where's the family headquarters in this town?'

'Aw shit, I just can't give you that, Bolan. That's too much, I could never live with myself.'

Bolan watched him for a moment, then said, 'Okay, I guess you're right. Get going, Danno.'

'You're letting me go?'

'A deal's a deal. Goodbye, Danno.'

'You're not, uh, going to shoot me in the back, Bolan.'

'You know better.' Bolan removed the clip from the *Uzi* and jammed it into his pouch. 'Just go on.'

The *caporegime* could hardly believe his good luck. He struggled to his feet and said, 'I ain't really told you anything to be ashamed of.'

'You bet you haven't,' Bolan assured him.

'Uh, look Bolan. You're not all that rotten. I mean, no offense, I didn't mean it that way. I just mean I wish you'd been with us all along, instead of against us.'

'War is like that, Danno,' Bolan said tiredly. 'Now go on. Next time we meet, one of us will probably come out of it dead.'

'Just the same, I'm not forgetting how straight you are,' Giliamo told him. He stepped to the edge of the stage and leapt off, turned to stare back at Bolan briefly, then hurried off into the night.

Bolan murmured to himself, 'I'm not all that straight, Danno.' He put the clip back in the *Uzi*, went down the steps and returned to the car. His outer garments were lying across the back seat. Affectionately he patted the little submachine gun, knowing that he would not be using it again, and lay it on the rear floor, then he quietly began getting into his clothing.

It was shaping into a hell of a war, he was thinking. How was a guy supposed to separate the good guys from the bad. If the *Mafiosi* were not responsible for the torture death of old Edwin Charles, then who the hell was? And for what possible motive?

He was wishing that he had never become involved with the Sades. But he had. And things were getting pretty badly entangled. Instinctively he knew that Danno had finally levelled with him. Bolan had taken all of the ham out of him as Stevie Carbon – Danno Giliamo had been talking straight. He was sure of that. So what did it all mean? That Ann Franklin's foster father was a rat? And if it should turn out that way, what would this mean to the girl? And what would it all mean to Bolan and to his ability to get the hell out of the country?

Yeah, it was getting tangled. Very soon now he would have to be doing something toward a firm identification of friend and foe. And then there was Charles. Bolan had liked the old man, even if the acquaintance had been microscopically brief. Living as Bolan did, you learned to take your likes quick, and he had definitely taken to the old soldier.

So somewhere along the tangled threads Bolan meant to identify a sadistic killer, and he meant to see that justice was done.

Right now, though, more pressing business was demanding his attention. He completed his dressing and sent the Lincoln rolling silently back through the park, lights out and prowling on the scent of an ex-POW.

Bolan spotted him on the third pass, huffing along on foot down the west perimeter of the park. The slightly overweight *Mafiosi* was making better time than Bolan had expected. He ran the Lincoln into a stand of shrubbery, quietly said goodbye to it, and closed in on the prey on foot, taking up the stalk at a proper distance.

No, Bolan was not all that straight. There was more than one way to extract intelligence from an enemy. Whether he knew it or not, Danno was not yet entirely free and the interrogation was still underway.

And the Executioner was closing on the enemy camp. The Assault on Soho, Stage Two, was in progress.

CHAPTER THIRTEEN

THE MEET

THE house was one of those inner London rarities, with a lawn, a courtyard, and an iron fence encircling the whole thing. Off to the side was a portico and a huge circular drive that could probably take a fairsized funeral procession. In better days it had probably been the townhouse of some nobleman; now it served as the local business hub and visitor center for the most powerful crime syndicate in history. And it was within easy walking distance of the neon wonderland of Piccadilly, but a hell of a long walk from Regents Park. Giliamo had apparently been in no great hurry to get back. Although the subway trains in London cease operation after midnight, there were still buses and taxicabs ... and the Mafia underboss had spurned them all, staying with his feet.

This was fine with Bolan; it made his task much easier. Maybe, he thought, the long walk was Giliamo's idea of penance for his imagined sins against the family. Or maybe he was just walking off a sense of anger and frustration and humiliation. Humiliated he had certainly been. Bolan knew the writhings of psyche required for a high ranking *Mafioso* to bargain for his life with the likes of a Mack Bolan.

Whatever the reasons, the journey from Regents Park back to Soho was a long and tiring one, consuming most of the early morning hours, and made worse by Giliamo's obvious unfamiliarity with the streets of London. He did a lot of doubling back and circling, dipping down to within sight of Piccadilly Circus before orienting himself into the final beeline to the house with the iron fence. During this last leg, Bolan noted that Danno was limping and moving along with more and more difficulty. Blisters, Bolan diagnosed. He had to smile at that. Blisters on the heel were armor for the soul, or so they'd told him in the army.

Now Bolan stood in the darkness across from the big house and wondered what was going on inside there. Every room in the place was ablaze with lights and vehicles were lined up in the circular drive inside the gates. A group of men stood under bright porchlights, another smaller group idled near the vehicles.

As Giliamo ascended the steps to the porch, Bolan heard a loud greeting of, 'Hey Danno, where the hell you been?'

A swirl of conversation hummed across the darkness to Bolan's stakeout position, then the group on the porch went inside with Giliamo. Another man came out a few minutes later and lit a cigarette. He called down some barely audible instructions to the men at the vehicles. That group promptly melted and the men went to separate cars. Then the man on the porch called out something else in a half-chiding tone – it sounded to Bolan like, 'The gates, the gates!'

The man in the lead vehicle leapt out and trotted down to open the large iron gate of the driveway, then hurried back to his car.

The man on the porch called, 'Don't worry, I'll get 'em behind you.'

The motorcade pulled out and Bolan drew back to avoid the headlamps as the line of vehicles swerved into the street and headed toward Piccadilly. As the last car cleared, the guy from the porch was walking down the drive toward the gate. Instead of closing it immediately, however, he stepped on through and stood on the sidewalk, gazing up and down the street. He threw the cigarette down and stepped on it, then put another between his lips and casually lit it, allowing the lighter to flame for an overlong time, putting his features in stark relief from the darkness.

Bolan's soul stirred in the recognition of that face over there. It belonged to Leo Turrin, the double-life *Mafioso* and undercover cop from Pittsfield. Once Bolan had been sworn to execute the cocky little Italian, whom he had known then only as the vice lord of Bolan's home town, and it had been through that involvement that Bolan had first successfully penetrated the Cosa Nostra and learned so much of their operation. Bolan had worked closely with Turrin during those early days at Pittsfield and had found himself growing more and more reluctant to collect his 'blood debt' from this likeable little guy. As things had turned out at Pittsfield, of course, Bolan had plenty of reason to be thankful that the Turrin execution had never come off. The guy had saved Bolan's skin more than once – and then, of course, he had turned out to be an undercover cop.

Now this glimpse of a face from the past was received with mixed emotions. Leo lived in the same brand of constant peril as Bolan's. The slightest hint that Turrin was enjoying friendly relations with the Executioner could mean his immediate undoing, and the loss of a five year undercover operation. Also, on the other side of the coin, Bolan was not all that certain that, with all chips down, Turrin would not hesitate to sacrifice Bolan to the greater good. Cops were like that, sometimes, even good cops.

Bolan's inner conflict was resolved much quicker than the telling of it, however. He ejected a bullet from the Beretta and tossed it across the street to land at Turrin's feet. The little guy bent over and picked it up, hefted it casually in his palm, glanced up the driveway toward the house, then unhurriedly crossed the street.

Bolan stepped out of the shadows, smiling faintly, and said, 'Why didn't you just light up a neon sign?'

They solemnly shook hands. Turrin gave Bolan his cigarette and told him, 'I figured you'd be somewhere close by – just a hunch. What'd you do to poor Danno? He looks like he's been to hell and back.'

'He has. What brings you to London?'

'You.'

Bolan chuckled. 'It figures. They calling in the reserves now?'

Turrin nodded. 'And more. Don't laugh when I tell you this. I'm supposed to be bringing you a pardon.'

Bolan did laugh. 'A what?'

'You heard me. They want to bury the hatchet.'

'Yeah, right in my head,' Bolan said.

'They're serious about it. I *think*. I believe Staccio has his doubts, secretly though.'

'*Joe* Staccio, upper New York?'

'Right. He's heading up the peace delegation. He's a little worried that the other bosses are setting him up for something. You know how that crap goes, none of them really trust each other.'

Bolan said, 'Yeah. Well, so what's your role in all this?'

Turrin grinned. 'They haven't forgotten that you used to be one of my boys. They figured I could make the contact. By the way, have you heard? I'm running Pittsfield now.'

Bolan chuckled and said, 'Congratulations, that's some territory. No more girls, eh?'

Turrin laughed softly and stiffened his hand into a flat plane and tipped it from side to side. 'I still keep my hand in,' he said. 'They'll never let me forget it anyway. I've got a new name, you know.'

'No, I didn't know.'

'They call me Leo Pussy.'

'It's a name that should stick,' Bolan commented, grinning.

'Yeah,' Turrin said drily. 'Well, so what are you up to? I mean, other than terrorizing the continent and bringing the blitz back to Britain?'

'I've just been trying to get home,' Bolan soberly told him. 'But I'm starting to smell something very rotten here in jolly old England. I think I might look around some.'

'By look, you mean blast.'

'Maybe that, too.'

'Look, you better cool it a bit. These London cops are something else. You remember Hal Brognola?'

'The Justice Department guy, yeah.'

'Right. Listen, Brognola packs a lot of weight. He takes no shit off of anybody, not even the boys up in Senate Judiciary. He's been trying to make some intercessions on your behalf with the local fuzz. No dice, buddy. They told him in plain text to jolly well butt the hell out.'

'So what's Brognola's interest?'

'You know how he feels about you. He figures you're performing a national service, and I hear there's considerable unofficial sympathy with his view. But that's Fed level, understand. There's not much he can do at the local levels, especially with you blitzing around. More to the point, though, Brognola's been trying to engineer a line on this London arm for months now. Zero, buddy, not a damn thing. And I couldn't help. I mean, I've got no right to know what's going on over here, right? So this trip was a blessing, in Hal's view. This is the first time we've gotten inside underground London.'

'Have you caught the smell yet?'

'What smell?'

'The rotten smell I was talking about. If this thing does bust, I've been told that this whole country might shake from the explosion.'

'Local corruption?'

'No, worse than that, from a public point of view. It could be the Profumo thing all over again, times ten and in spades.'

Turrin said, 'Shit.'

'Yeah. That could be why Scotland Yard is so hardnosed. Maybe they know that smell already, and they're afraid it's going to bust wide open.'

'I doubt that,' Turrin replied worriedly. 'The C.I.D. has a hell of a lot of pride. They're just not going to let you run wild over here, that's all.'

Bolan said, 'Well, we'd better cut this short. What can I do to help your operation?'

Turrin produced a small notebook, jotted a phone number, and tore out the sheet and handed it to Bolan. 'Contact me here, sometime today if you can. We'll work out a meet.'

'Okay. Where were all the cars headed?'

'Airport. Arnie Farmer Castiglione is bringing in a big head party, due to land at six. Staccio insisted that we come on ahead and try to get a jump on them. But nobody's been home here all night and hell, we've just been sitting around waiting for someone to show.'

'What do you mean, get a jump?'

Turrin grinned. 'It's the big squeeze, buddy. Peace in one hand and war in the other. If we make contact first, meaning the peace delegation, the Farmer is supposed to lay off and give us a chance to work something out.'

'But you think he won't.'

'Right, that's the feeling. But we're supposed to give it the old college try. For what it's worth, Staccio brought with him the full authority of the *Commissione* to make a deal with you.'

'Castiglione's on that *Commissione*.'

'Right. But you know how these things go. The old warrior hates your guts, Sarge.'

Bolan shrugged. 'So, old warriors die too, you know.'

Turrin said, 'Yeah, you could look at it that way, I guess. Listen, I don't really know all the details ... Staccio's playing this thing pretty close to the chest. I'm just supposed to make the contact and set up the meet. Maybe you should listen to what he has to say. It might be your out.'

'Who says I want an out?'

Turrin smiled faintly. 'You can't keep this going forever, Sarge.'

Bolan grinned and said, 'I can try.'

'Well ... okay. It's your decision. Hell don't look to me for advice, of all people. Uh, you need anything from me that doesn't come under that heading?'

'I could use some intelligence.'

'I'll do what I can. What do you need?'

'I need a make on an old man named Edwin Charles, age about seventy or seventy-five. I think he was a biggie in OSS liaison during World War Two. Maybe someone can get a line from that angle. He died tonight.'

Turrin said, 'Friend or foe?'

'That's what I'm hoping you can tell me.'

'Okay. I have a line to Brognola. I'll put him on it.'

'While you're at it, look into a Major Mervyn Stone. The major part is a carryover, he's not active military anymore. The name's all I have, but there is a connection with Charles.'

'Pretty important stuff, Sarge?'

'Yeah, pretty important. My head might be attached to it.'

'Okay, we'll shake the tree. You watch it, huh?'

Turrin moved casually back across the street, pulled the gate shut, and walked up the drive whistling a pop tune.

Bolan watched him out of sight, then faded away into the night.

That was a good cop back there, a damn good cop. Bolan wished him long life. But he feared a short one for him. Perhaps as short as Bolan's own.

CHAPTER FOURTEEN

THE PACT

ANOTHER night had all but ended when Bolan returned to Russell Square. Lights were on here and there inside Queen's House and a faint illumination marked the rectangle of Ann Franklin's window. After a cautious recon, Bolan went in through the rear entrance and let himself into the flat with the key the girl had given him.

Ann was waiting for him. She was in a chair directly facing the door, she was entirely awake, and she was holding the big Weatherby in a tense grip and pointing it right at his belly button.

He closed the door and asked her, 'Forgotten me already?'

'I haven't forgotten you,' she replied coldly.

'What are you doing with my rifle?'

'Protecting myself.'

'Against me?'

She tipped her head in a deliberate nod. 'Against you.'

Bolan tried a grin that didn't quite come off. 'Is it all right with you, Lady Gunner, if I have a cigarette?'

'If that means may you reach inside your jacket, no, you may not.'

Bolan did not like a bit of this. He said, 'Look, I'm not feeling up to games. Don't believe it about an infantryman's feet. They get as tender as anybody's, and I've been on mine all night. Now what's going on?'

She murmured, 'Thank goodness your tender feet are no concern of mine.'

He said, 'Forget the feet, it's tough shoulders that count. Particularly the gun shoulder. When those big pieces go off they buck into you like an enraged bull. I've known guys to come off the firing line with fractured collarbones.'

'I've handled firearms before,' she assured him.

Bolan did not like the icy stare she was giving him. He wondered, but would not ask, where Major Stone was at the moment. He said, 'Where have you handled firearms? On the clay pigeon line?' He shook his head. 'That's no pop gun you're holding there, Lady Gunner. It was made to deliver a killing punch at better than a thousand yards. That's three thousand feet, better than half a mile, or roughly one kilometer, to put it in your terms. That kind of killing power requires a muzzle energy of more than four thousand pounds – that's where the enraged bull comes from – and it takes a bullet of at least 300 grains. No military style steel jackets on those jobbies, either. That Weatherby is a big game rifle, meaning the bullets are blunt-nose expanders, designed for high shocking power. They mushroom on impact, and they tear through like a small bomb. You pop me with that charge from where you're sitting and you'll be cleaning pieces of me off of every wall in the room, and maybe even some out in the hall. If you want to try for something really gory, then lay it in right between my eyes. You might get some scrambled brains clear into your frying pan. Or if—'

'That will be quite enough of that,' she interrupted. Her face had gone white and a nervous tic was beginning to work at the corner of her mouth.

Bolan said, 'I think so, too. So if you really mean to shoot me, then why don't you put the clip in?'

'The what?'

'The ammo clip. Why didn't you load the gun?'

A distressed look crossed her face. She said, 'Oh,' and glanced down at the rifle.

Bolan stepped forward and took it away from her.

'How stupid of me,' she murmured.

'Not at all,' Bolan said solemnly. 'As a matter of fact, it is loaded. This piece doesn't use a clip.' He pulled the bolt and ejected a long wicked looking bullet. It whizzed past the girl's face and struck the floor with a heavy clatter. 'That's a magnum,' he explained, 'and it has a hell of a lot more than 300 grains.'

She winced and stared at the shell as though spellbound by it.

He told her, 'You know, I'm getting just a bit fed up with your whole nutty bunch.'

'Obviously,' she replied in a small voice.

'Now just what does that mean?'

Her lip quivered and she said, 'I told you that Charles was harmless. There was really no need at all to kill him. It was wanton and violent and . . . and inexcusable.'

Bolan's face showed his disgust with her. He said, 'Lady, if you think I killed that poor old man then you're clear off your pole.'

He carried the rifle into the bedroom and began snatching his things out of the closet. He was stuffing the Weatherby into its case when the girl appeared in the doorway.

She said, 'Mack . . .' in a soft voice.

He turned a harsh glare on her. Her eyes faltered and she slowly entered the room to stand uneasily at the foot of the bed. Bolan was thinking that she had performed that exact same maneuver the night before, and he had to wonder if it was sheer coincidence.

Gruffly, he told her, 'Okay, so maybe you had a right to think it. You're right, I am a killer. In fact, I killed about a dozen men tonight, maybe two. Hell, I don't even bodycount anymore. But I don't murder doddering old men by bending them over a hot iron. That's not exactly cricket in my circles, lady. Yours, maybe, but not mine.'

She flinched and softly replied, 'All right, I deserved that. Now will you forgive me?'

'I already did.' He was carelessly throwing his things into the suitcase. 'But it's time I was moving on. Too long in one spot makes me nervous. Thanks, and all that.' He snapped the bag shut and dropped it to the floor, then finished securing-in the Weatherby.

'Where will you go?'

'I'll find something.'

'There's really no need for all this, you know. You're perfectly welcome to remain here.'

'It's better that I don't,' he assured her.

'Then you're just ditching us, leaving us all alone to solve an impossible problem, and after all we've done to help you.'

Quietly, Bolan said, 'That's right, you've helped a lot, haven't you. You brought me to an ambush in Dover, then you brought me to an ambush in Soho, not once but twice. You people keep helping me, Ann, and you're going to help me right into a grave.'

She took a deep breath, let it all out, and said, 'If you didn't kill Charles, then who did?'

Bolan's eyes clashed with hers. He sat down on the edge of the bed and lit a cigarette, then muttered, 'I wish I knew.'

She said, 'He died hideously. I was there, I saw it. The C.I.D. was there also. And I'm under technical arrest.'

'What does that mean?'

'It means that I'm not to leave London until the investigation is completed. It's a technicality. C.I.D. is convinced that you are the murderer. They seem to think that the museum is part of a Mafia racket. They think that you tortured Charles to get information out of him, then when the gangsters came, you killed them all in a shootout.'

Bolan grunted and said, 'It figures. I guess I'd be thinking along those same lines if I were a cop.' He took a long pull at the cigarette and slowly exhaled. 'Actually,' he said thoughtfully, 'I was hung up on the same kind of error, at first. I automatically concluded that the *Mafiosi* killed the old man. That tied everything into a neat bundle, see.'

She shook her head. 'No, I don't see. What do you mean?'

'Well, you stop thinking of motives and that sort of thing the minute you settle for a gang killing. But I'm convinced now that the mob didn't do it. And I didn't do it. So that takes us back to *who* and *why* – and especially the *why*. You tell me, Ann. *Why* was Charles killed?'

The girl sat down beside Bolan, clasped her hands between her knees, and stared broodingly at the floor. 'I haven't the foggiest,' she said, sighing.

He asked her, '*Is* that museum part of a Mafia racket?'

Her eyelids fluttered as she replied, 'Only in the way that I've already explained. We are being blackmailed.'

'So how did Charles figure into that angle?'

Her lips quivered. She leaned against Bolan and told him, 'He was simply a sweet old love who enjoyed puttering

about with electronics. Actually he was more of a main-
tenance electrician than anything else. Charles had abso-
lutely no connection with any of the club's business.'

'He didn't operate that peepshow console in the
basement?'

'It's largely self-operative. Charles merely saw to it.'

'Did Charles install the cameras and the other gadgets?'

'Install them?' She shook her head. 'Oh no, not the orig-
inal equipment. That was all done quite some time before
Charles came to us.'

'And when did he come to you?'

She wrinkled her brow and replied, 'Some months back.
Three, perhaps four.'

'Was that before or after the blackmail started?'

'Oh it was after. I'm positive of that. It was because of
that trouble that the Major decided to have a full time
watchman about the place. Charles lived in, you see. Had his
own flat in the cellar.'

'And how did the Major happen to pick Charles for the
job?'

Her eyes blanked and she said, 'I haven't the foggiest
notion.'

Bolan sighed and stretched toward the night stand to
crush the cigarette into an ashtray. When he straightened,
Ann was lying back on the bed, her legs dangling over the
edge. He stared at her for a thoughtful moment, then told
her, 'I've no intention of ditching you, Ann.'

'Thanks,' she replied in a half whisper. 'But I'm releasing
you. You have no obligations to me.'

'It isn't a matter of obligation,' he said.

Her face took on a warm glow. Her eyes half closed and
she whispered, 'It isn't?'

He shook his head. 'Uh-uh. It's a matter of safety. Yours.
Whoever did it to Charles might decide to do it to you,
too.'

'Why me?' she gasped.

He shrugged. 'Why Charles?'

She said, 'But that's ridiculous!' Her face, though, showed
that the idea was not entirely ridiculous.

'Just what is your job at *de Sade*?' Bolan asked her.

She closed her eyes and flung an arm across the top of her head. One foot came up on the bed and she wriggled about in discomfort.

Bolan said, 'Dammit, it's important. Now what do you do over there?'

'I plan the parties,' she replied, her voice barely audible. 'I stage the shows and see to the decorations and make arrangements for the food and beverages. I am in complete charge of all party arrangements.'

Bolan said, 'What's involved in staging a show?'

'Many things,' she replied listlessly. 'Foremost is a thorough understanding of the members' various idiosyncrasies. First I must determine precisely which members will be attending. Then I simply build the show around the sort of things that give them enjoyment.'

'Where do you get the actors?'

'They're a repertory company, under contract to the club. They are well paid and quite content with the working conditions. Also some of them, I suspect, have idiosyncrasies of their own.'

'How about you?'

'What?'

'Idiosyncrasies.'

Her face flamed. 'I have a huge one.'

'Tell me.'

She sighed. Her eyes remained closed and she said, 'Utter revulsion. I find the entire thing abominable and revolting.'

'Then why do you stick on with it?'

Following a long silence, she replied, 'I once thought that I stayed because of the Major. We're not exactly a father and daughter item, you know, nothing like that. I believe that the Major is constitutionally unsuited for the father role. But he did take over my upbringing when my aunt died. He's a very cold man, as you may have noticed, but he does have a sense of duty. I suppose that he instilled that in me, also. He saw to my problems for a number of years. I suppose that, when I came of age, I felt a need to see to his problems. But the Major released me last year ... even *asked* me to go ... so I haven't that excuse to fall back on any more, have I?'

'So what are you saying?' Bolan probed on.

She came up to one elbow, tossed her head to one side, and opened her eyes to fix them on Bolan. 'I'm saying that I don't know why I stay on. Perhaps I have become fixated on abomination and revulsion.' She looked away from him then and asked, 'Do you find me revolting?'

'Not at all,' he murmured.

'I'm a damn virgin, did you know that?'

It was time for Bolan to look the other way. He was curiously embarrassed by the admission. 'No, I hadn't noticed,' he muttered.

'And I'm twenty-six years in this world. Now isn't *that* some sort of an anachronism in this flaming age.' She said it quite bitterly.

Bolan wanted to leave the subject. He said, 'Did you stage the show for last night's party?'

'Yes.'

'Did it include a torture scene in the cell where Charles died?'

Her eyes flared as she replied, 'Yes, but not *that* one.'

'What was scheduled for that room?'

'Jimmy Thomas.'

'And what is Jimmy Thomas?'

Her face again flamed. She said, 'Jimmy Thomas is a sodomist . . . a – a passive, a vessel.'

'I don't get you.'

She had to close her eyes to explain. 'He – he . . . well, you saw the device, I'm sure. He bends himself into the locks and . . . receives.'

Bolan's mouth was dry. He said, 'Yeah. So why wasn't Jimmy Thomas in there receiving, instead of the old man?'

She explained, 'The Major said that he'd received a request from one of the members to . . . to . . .'

'To do what?'

'One of the members desired Jimmy's personal company during the party.'

'And when was this?'

'At the last moment, I suppose. I had to leave early. Remember, I was meeting you at Soho Psych.'

'Supposedly the Major was, too,' Bolan pointed out.

'He was there,' she said. 'He told me that he knocked into you just outside the dining room.'

Bolan said, 'Yeah, about twenty minutes late.'

'But he said that he'd explained that to you. The gangsters were following him. He was trying to shake them loose.'

Bolan decided that he did not wish to tell her differently, not at the moment. He sighed and asked her, 'Just how emotionally attached are you to Major Stone, Ann?'

She replied, 'Not at all. I've explained all that, I'd thought.'

He said, 'Suppose it turns out that Major Stone is the one who killed the old man.'

Her eyelashes fluttered rapidly. 'That's preposterous.'

'Is it?'

'Utterly.'

'Well just for the sake of argument, suppose he did. How would you feel about that?'

Her voice dropped into low key again as she said, 'Then I would fear that he had gone quite mad. I would feel the deepest pity for him.'

'If he did do it, Ann, I'll probably have to zap him.'

'You'll have to what?'

'There's something smelly about this whole setup, and I'm not talking about sexual perversion. Something very rotten and very evil is underlying this entire mish-mash, and I'm betting that Edwin Charles did not die at some madman's spur of the moment whim. He died for some damn good reason. I believe that this reason somehow is related to my presence in London, and I'm betting that the killer and I will have a showdown before it's all over. When that happens, Ann, I will probably kill him.'

She murmured, 'And you believe that this shadowy "someone" could possibly be Major Stone.'

'It's more than a possibility,' he told her.

The girl pulled herself erect. She crossed her legs, Indian fashion as she sat on the bed. She gazed steadily at Bolan for a thoughtful moment, then said, 'But suppose that Charles was actually in on the blackmail plot?'

'That could change things,' Bolan admitted. 'Do you think he was?'

She shrugged her shoulders. 'I hardly know what to think at this point.' She got off the bed and went to the window, pulled back the blinds, and stared somberly outside. 'It's daylight,' she announced quietly. 'What a difference twenty-four hours can bring.'

Bolan wanted to get things firmly understood. He told her, 'The point of it all, Ann ... I may turn out to be your very worst enemy.'

'You could never be that,' she murmured, still gazing out the window.

'A few minutes ago you were ready to blow my head off,' he reminded her.

'Not really.' She sighed and her head drooped toward the windowpane. 'I was simply shocked and frightened and confused. I could never have pulled that trigger. I'm in love with you, Mack.'

Bolan said, 'All right, maybe I feel something of the same for you. But it won't change a thing at the nitty-gritty level, Ann. I'm going to keep hacking at this thing, and the chips are going to lie where they fall.'

Silent tears were oozing down the smooth cheeks as she turned to him and said, 'Then let's make a pact.'

'What sort of pact?' he asked gruffly.

'To love one another ... 'til murder do us part.'

He said, 'Dammit, Ann,' and moved to her and took her in his arms.

She gave way entirely then, the sobs racking her and the tears flowing unrestrained. Bolan held her and patted her and whispered, 'Hey, hey, hey ...'

She had her cry, and a tender kiss or two, and she was nuzzling contentedly at his shoulder when suddenly she stiffened and raised her head to gaze intently out the window.

'Mack!' she said, her voice tight with alarm. 'You said you've been afoot ... but ... did a taxi cab bring you here?'

He followed her gaze to the window and replied, 'Yes, but I had him drop me up on Euston Road. What's going on out there?'

'Did I forget to ...? Charles warned me that the taxi

companies were alerted to watch out for you. Now see what . . .'

Bolan grabbed the blinds and closed them with a jerk. Russell Square was beginning to crawl with bobbies. He flung himself away from the girl and snatched up the gun-case and headed for the door.

Ann grabbed his suitcase and ran after him.

'You stay!' he commanded.

'I'll not stay,' she repplied firmly. 'I've a rental car in the alley. Don't waste time arguing.'

Bolan knew the wisdom of that last remark. He quickly doused the lights and grabbed Ann's elbow and hustled her through the doorway and along to the rear stairway.

With a lot of luck, they just might make it. 'Listen,' he said urgently, 'if the cops start shooting, then that's it and it's the end of things. You hit the dirt and dammit don't move a muscle. And you tell 'em that I was holding a gun on you. Remember that, you were my prisoner – otherwise they'll throw the book at you.'

'We'll escape,' she said confidently. 'Never worry, we'll get through.'

She was plucky as hell and Bolan was proud of her and . . . yeah, he was more than just proud of her.

He hadn't really wanted to leave her behind. They'd made a pact. They were together until . . . Bolan was hoping for a long romance. But, under the circumstances, he was not counting on it.

CHAPTER FIFTEEN

DOUBLE DUPLICITY

GILIAMO and Turrin were outside to greet the new arrivals as the glistening motorcade swept into the drive. Staccio had remained in the house, growling, 'If Arnie Farmer wants to see me, let 'im look me up.'

As the vehicles continued to pull in, Giliamo leaned back toward Turrin and remarked, 'Christ, how many heads has he brought with him?'

Turrin grinned. 'You ain't seen nothing. This is just his personal party. We made arrangements around town for the other crews.'

The driver of the lead vehicle jumped out and snatched open the rear door. A loud command from inside resulted in the door being hastily closed again. The driver ran down the line of vehicles, thumping doors and issuing orders on the run. Men began erupting from the cars and milling about in confusion until crew leaders took over and turned the chaos into order. Two groups went to the street, broke up, and disappeared. Others began prowling the grounds and manning the fence. Another group filed solemnly past Giliamo and Turrin with hardly a glance at the reception committee and went inside, presumably to shake down the house.

Turrin had watched all this with a bemused smile. In a low aside to Giliamo, he remarked, 'Talk about your palace guard. The President should have such a security thing, eh?'

Giliamo, though, was obviously impressed by the show of force. He said, 'Look I don't blame 'im. I know. I been there.'

'You been where?'

The Jerseyite flushed and replied, 'Never mind, I know all about this Bolan and I gotta hand it to Arnie Farmer, he knows what he's doing.'

Turrin chuckled and watched the proceedings without further comment. Presently a hard-looking man approached the Castiglione vehicle, quietly opened the door, and said something to the men inside in a hushed voice. Two body-guards exited from the front seat, on the opposite side, and took up waiting positions there, looking nervously around. Another two came off the jumpseats in the rear and brack-eted the doorway with their bodies. Then the man himself stepped out, followed quickly by a companion. The body-guards fell in to form a tight circle and the party moved forward with Castiglione barely visible in the center.

As they were ascending the steps, Turrin muttered to Gi-liamo, 'Now don't forget and call 'im Arnie.'

Giliamo nodded and stepped forward with a big smile. 'Glad to see you, Mr. Castiglione,' he called out. 'Christ, things have been going to hell over here. I'm sure glad to see you.' Then the smile faded, and Danno pulled on a shocked face. Nick Trigger was standing there beside the great man, and he also was wearing a dumbfounded look.

Castiglione was giving Giliamo a thoughtful glare. He said, 'I'm glad to see you too, Danno. Nick's been telling me all about your fuckin' head getting blown off.'

Giliamo said, 'Christ, I thought the same about him! For Christ's sake, Nick, how'd you get out of that?'

Nick smiled pastily and glanced at Arnie Farmer. 'I don't know,' he mumbled. 'I think I got my brains rattled a little.'

'I think somebody's got something rattled,' Castiglione growled. 'Let's talk about it inside. This's the lousiest weather I ever saw, Danno. Is it always like this over here?'

Turrin recognized the weather-talk as a subtle shift of favor from Nick Trigger to Danno.

Giliamo had picked it up also. He replied, 'It's been pretty bad. They got a pollution problem, I think, but then who hasn't. And it mixes with the damned fog I guess, and you gotta wear warmer clothes than that, Mr. Castiglione, that'll never do over here, you'll catch your death o' cold.'

They went on past Leo Turrin with only a glance and a nod of the head from Arnie Farmer. Turrin nodded back and watched them go inside, and he was thinking that Danno was a Mafia politician to watch. Disarmingly frank and open, all smiles – and all the while probably, a switchblade concealed in his fist.

The man who had been driving the Castiglione vehicle came slowly up the steps and stood beside Turrin. Leo gave him a cigarette and they both lit up. The driver exhaled and said disgustedly, 'Big fuckin' deal.'

Turrin grinned and told him, 'Maybe you'll be Capo some day, Wheeler.'

'No way,' the wheelman replied. 'Not if I gotta act like that. That turns my stomach, Leo.'

Toby Wheeler was a member of Turrin's crew from Pittsfield. The name was obviously a Mafia monicker, but Leo had never heard any other used on the man. The story went that Wheeler had once been a racing car driver and twice had narrowly missed qualifying for the big one at Indianapolis. Now he was a valuable chauffeur, a wheelman *par excellence*. He sucked again on the cigarette and told his boss, 'I got to take that Caddie back to the U-Drive, Leo. It's pulling a little to the left in the turns. They shouldn't check out faulty equipment like that.'

Turrin nodded and said, 'Okay, I'll tell you when. Right now I want a report. What was Arnie talking about on the way in?'

'This'n that, mostly that. Buncha shit, really. All about what he's going to do to this Bolan bastard. And that other guy . . . what's his name?'

'Nick Trigger.'

'Yeah, that Nick Trigger . . . did you see his face when he spotted Danno? He was out at the airport on his own, to meet the planes. Do you know what he was talking about most of the way in here? He was telling Arnie the Pig all about how Danno had fucked up everything over here, just everything, and about how Danno wound up walking into a Bolan trap and getting hisself splattered all over some street.'

Turrin smiled and commented, 'So that's what it was.'

'Yeah, and did you hear the first thing Danno says to Nick? He says for Christ's sake, how'd Nick get out of that. How did *Nick* get out. And Nick had been telling Arnie the Pig that he wouldn't go with Danno because he knew Danno was all fucked up. He told him that flat out, I heard it.'

'You better go easy on that Arnie the Pig stuff,' Turrin advised quietly.

'With all due respect to the good bosses, Leo, that's what he is. But you're right, I better go easy on it. I hear he took a territory away from a boy once just because the guy forgot to call him *mister*. Imagine that. Next he'll be wanting to be called *Don* Castiglione. Listen, Leo, I'd rather not wheel for Arnie if you can get someone else.'

Turrin chuckled. 'Don't worry, Arnie will be rolling with his own wheelman from here on. You was just a courtesy. Say, is that all you got to tell me?'

'Naw, you were right, they're planning something. They were talking careful because they know I'm with you. And I couldn't put my finger on any one thing they said, but I know shit when I hear it. Take my word, Leo, they're planning something.'

'Okay thanks, Wheeler.' Turrin squeezed the man's arm and went on inside to join the others. Leo knew damn well they were planning something. But that was okay. Leo knew how to make plans too.

It seemed that the park at Russell Square was being used as a marshalling point for the police. Bolan could hear the sharp commands and sound of running feet as the squads split off into their search areas. He had agreed that Ann would pilot the car; she slid in behind the wheel as Bolan put his things in and dived into the back seat.

A uniformed policeman ran into view and cried, 'Hold on there!' – but the car had already begun to move and was picking up momentum in a quick plunge down the alley.

Whistles were sounding back there, and a sudden swirl of blue suits in the area they had just vacated revealed to Bolan the narrowness of their escape. And they were not all that clear yet.

The little car swerved into the street below Russell Square

and skidded off into an easterly run. Bolan threw a leg over and fought his way into the front seat as a tootling wail of sirens rose up to plague their rear. He asked the girl, 'Do you know where you're going?'

'Not just yet,' she gasped. 'Never worry, they'll not catch us.'

Bolan could believe it. She was an expert driver, and she was pushing the car to the limit of the terrain, zig-zagging through the London maze in a way that would make downstream interceptions very unlikely. After several minutes of this it became evident that they had gotten away. The sounds of pursuit became fainter and more confused, and Bolan told her, 'You're some wheelman.'

'It's my first time,' she admitted, the dark eyes flashing with excitement. 'I mean, very nearly.'

They were running easy now, angling toward the Thames and slowly working into a westward swing. The town seemed fully awakened, and the streets were becoming choked with buses and private vehicles as the off-to-work crowd descended on the inner city.

The girl told Bolan, 'I believe I've decided where we shall go.'

'And where is that?'

'Soho Psych, for now. We'll spend a few hours there, until things cool off a bit, then we'll be off to Brighton. I've a cottage there. And it will be a perfectly smashing place.'

Never mind smashing Brighton, Bolan's mind was still hung up on that first place. His eyes narrowed somewhat and he echoed, 'Soho Psych?'

'Yes, there'll be nobody about but the cleaning personnel – and surely no one would think to look for you there. Then the cottage in Brighton will make an ideal layover. We'll keep you concealed there until we can find a way to smuggle you out of the country.'

'Wait just a minute,' he growled. 'What's the deal on Soho Psych? I don't know that I—'

She interrupted with a peal of nervous laughter. 'How rotten of me, I assumed you knew. The Psych is my place, at least half of it is.'

'Who owns the other half?' he asked darkly.

'Major Stone is my partner. But never worry, if you're still thinking of your dreadful suspicions. The Major rarely visits the place, he's what you would term a silent partner.'

The whole idea was a bit too overpowering for Bolan to assimilate immediately. He mulled the thing through his mind, finally growling, 'Okay, we'll try it.'

She smiled. 'I have a flat there. We shall be quite comfortable.'

'It seems that you have flats all over London,' he replied drily.

She tossed her head and said, 'Not really. The place back at Queen's House is merely a convenience for me. You'll never realize what a luxury absolute privacy can be until you've lived my life of the past few years. Sometimes I simply must get away from all of it. Queen's House is my getaway place.'

'Yes, you mentioned that,' he said, still watching narrowly.

'The flat at the club is another convenience, a business one though, I assure you. Frequently I'm there until all hours. It's nice to have a place to refresh one's self from time to time.'

'Uh-huh.' Bolan was not enjoying the thoughts that were crowding his mind. 'And, of course, you share another place with Major Stone.'

'Yes.' She looked at him and smiled. 'Cheer up. I just sleep there, and even that as seldom as possible. It's a matter of family, actually. I grew up in that house.'

'And then there's Brighton.'

'Yes, well, that's my weekender. Brighton is on the sea, you know. A very nice resort, really. I love it there, by the sea.'

They drove in silence for several minutes, during which time Bolan was attempting to organize his mind. They swung past Piccadilly and began angling into Soho. The big house with the iron gate slid past. Bolan noted that the vehicles had returned. He asked Ann, 'Who's place is that?' He wouldn't have been surprised to hear her identify it as the old family home.

She had sensed his hostility, and her own mood had suffered a marked deterioration also. Coolly, she replied, 'It once belonged to the Earl of—'

'I mean now. Who lives there now?'

She shook her head and told him, 'I haven't the foggiest.'

He almost grinned and said, 'You're sure of that?'

A smile hovered just beneath the surface of her lips. She murmured, 'Whatever is the matter with you? Honestly, you're the bloodiest, most suspicious person I have ever known.'

He sighed and told her, 'It keeps me breathing, kiddo.'

'Well, please don't start to get edgy with me. I've plans for you this beautiful morning.'

'What sort of plans?'

One hand dropped away from the steering wheel and found Bolan's in a warm grip. 'I'm going to ask you to prove something to me.'

'And what's that?' he asked, though he already suspected the answer.

'It's high time I discovered whether or not I'm a natural woman. Don't you think so?'

Bolan thought so. He murmured, 'Just so you know exactly what you're doing, Ann.'

'But I'm leaving all that to you,' she said, with what he was sure was a forced smile. She was an open gal, yeah, but she wasn't brassy. 'I intend to place myself entirely into your hands.'

Bolan was looking at her and visualizing all that entirely in his hands. Either he was the most fortunate man in London or the biggest sucker. He sighed and said, 'Wrong.'

'What?'

'It's the other way around, m'lady. I have placed myself entirely in *your* hands.'

She understood his meaning. She shivered slightly and said, 'Trust me, Mack.'

'I guess I have to,' he said solemnly. But not entirely. Bodies like that one had launched armadas, sure. They had also brought down Samsons and Caesars. No. Bolan would never be *entirely* in her hands. Or so he thought at the time.

CHAPTER SIXTEEN

PROOFS AND SYMBOLS

ANN FRANKLIN'S 'plans' for Bolan's morning seemed headed for a readjustment the moment they entered the club. There was a sizeable crowd in the bar, there was considerable churning about, and voices raised in loud argument were spilling into the entrance lobby. Several girls stood idly just outside the doorway to the bar, and these reacted to Ann's appearance there with noticeable good humor.

'Thank heaven you've arrived, Miss Franklin,' said a tall beauty in tight pants. 'Perhaps you could go in there and set that ruddy Donovan straight over our rest periods.'

Apparently they had walked in on a heated labor-management dispute.

'Some cleaning personnel,' Bolan remarked to Ann Franklin, looking the girls over in an overtly masculine appraisal. He knew better. The tight seated one who had addressed Ann was the blonde tube girl Bolan had seen the night before. He was wondering if Ann 'staged' the entertainment here, too. She murmured an excuse to Bolan and pushed into the bar with the girls. The blonde hung back at the door to send Bolan an over-the-shoulder examination, then she smiled and went on.

Bolan lit a cigarette and paced about the lobby, wondering what the hell was he doing there. Ann reappeared, looking flustered, and pressed a key into his hand. She pecked his cheek and told him, 'You may as well go on up. I'll be along as soon as possible. I've some trouble here.'

Bolan asked, 'Go on up where?'

She pointed out a drapery-concealed stairway at the end of the lobby, kissed his chin, and hurried back into the bar.

Bolan went up, with misgivings, and found a stunningly luxurious apartment. Here was no masculine austerity such as he had found at Queen's House. Persian carpets and oriental tapestries put him more in tune with the motif of the harem room at *Museum de Sade*, and the incidental decorations did little to refute that image.

Life-sized nudes, both sexes, dominated the walls and complemented a scattering of figurines and bronze castings of couples coupled in a variety of positions. Bolan whistled softly and went on through.

It was a single large room with a bed-in-the-round plat-form at dead center, raised several smooth steps above the rest of the place; like a stage, Bolan couldn't help thinking; and an Arabian Nights sunken bath just below with circular marble steps going down into a bubbling fountain pool which could cheerfully accommodate a fairsized guest list all at once. It was filled with water and some sort of rotating light arrangement set into the fountain was sending spark-ling psychedelic patterns all around.

A small kitchenette was thrown in, almost as an after-thought, and completing the arrangement were a well stocked bar and a tiny secretary shoved casually off to the side.

Yeah, Bolan decided, it would be a perfect spot to refresh one's self from time to time – any time. One half of his mind saw Ann Franklin fitting beautifully into the place; the other half saw her more naturally in Queen's House, at least a full world apart from the screamingly overt sexuality of this unbelievable pad. A virgin, eh?

So what could it all add up to, what could it possibly mean?

Bolan found a telephone at the center of the outrageous bed. He bounced gingerly on the soft fluff, then pulled the phone across by the cord and dialed the number Leo Turrin had given him.

It rang three times before a cautious voice responded with, 'Yeah?'

'Leo the Pussy,' Bolan growled.

'Just a minute.'

Bolan waited more than a minute. Then he heard the click

of an extension phone coming off the hook and Turrin's voice asked, 'Who's this?'

'You ast me to call you when you come in.'

'Oh. This th' iron man?'

'Right.'

'Say I can't talk to you right now, kid. We got a meeting going on.'

Bolan grinned into the mouthpiece. 'Well it's your show. But you better know, I don't have a lotta time. I'm about to get tied up on something myself.'

'Well, I'd like to talk to you, kid. How 'bout meeting me somewheres?'

'You name it,' Bolan replied.

'You know the Tower of London?'

'I can find it.'

'It's down by the Thames, down past London Bridge and, uh, let's see, like going down to th' docks. You got a picture?'

'Yeah, I'll find it. When?'

'Listen, meet me on Execution Row in about an hour.'

Bolan almost laughed into the telephone. He controlled himself and said, 'What's that Execution Row?'

'Aw, it's part of the sightseeing kick down there, it's where Ann Boleyn got hers, you know, a historical spot. Just ask a guide when you get there. Uh, kind of mix in with the tourists, you know, don't look obvious. I gotta talk to you about something important. It'll be worth something to you, don't worry.'

'Okay, in about an hour.'

'Uh, wait a minute. Somebody just told me it don't open 'til ten. Tell you what, meet me there at ten thirty.'

'Ten thirty it is,' Bolan agreed.

'Okay, and remember I said to don't look obvious. Nothing personal, kid, I mean I'm not ashamed of meeting you in the open, nothing like that. I just don't want no London cops busting me, you understand that.'

Bolan understood perfectly. 'Okay, and here's one for you, Leo. You come alone, nobody but you. I get nervous in a crowd.'

Turrin chuckled and said something in an aside to a third

person, then he told Bolan, 'Don't worry, I'll be alone. You just watch your end.'

Bolan growled a goodbye and hung up. It had been obvious that Turrin had been speaking in a crowd, probably from a table-top conference. Now he would be explaining to those listening that the call had come from a guy who could put him next to Bolan.

Okay, fine. So what happened if someone else at that table decided to get next to Bolan first? Bolan sighed. He would simply have to trust Turrin to handle that possibility.

It seemed that all of a sudden he was having to trust an awful hell of a lot of people to keep his head on. And Bolan didn't like it, not a bit. The jungle never saw after its own; in the jungle, survival was always an individual proposition.

A sound from across the room brought him out of his thoughts, and he looked up to see Ann Franklin quietly regarding him. He waved to her from the bed-stage-whatever and called down, 'It's a swinging pad. What's a nice girl like you doing with all this *schmazz*?'

She ascended the steps with a hesitant smile and said '*Schmazz*, is that good or bad?'

He shrugged and grinned at her. 'Depends on what ticks you,' he replied in the same light tone. 'Did you get your labor problem settled?'

She jerked her head in a curt nod and did something behind her to make her dress fall off.

Bolan's eyes flared at the spectacular view. She wore little bikini panties which were a mere technicality, and a no-bra bra that wasn't even that. His earlier recollection of the flawless skin proved valid, and even somewhat unfair. He had viewed it then through wearied and bloodshot eyes. Now they were neither weary nor bloodshot and the beauty of this woman was almost appalling. He said, 'Dammit, Ann!'

'I told you,' she murmured. 'I'm in your hands.'

He pulled her down beside him and she fell onto her back, curving around in a graceful sprawl with one knee slightly raised and both arms yoked up above her head. He touched her here and there, almost reverently, and she responded with a purring little sigh.

'Kiss me,' she whispered.

He did so, and found the inner man of him rising to mingle with the heady sensuality of the moment. Yeah, yeah – it could be love.

'Oh I love you, Mack,' she whispered, voicing the thing he could not.

He touched her again and she squirmed under the sensation, catching her breath and in a sharp intake and rising toward him for another soulful mingling of lips and teeth and tongue and all of it.

He got away from it, smiled, and asked her a hell of a question, all considered. 'You're sure this is what you want?'

She held his face with both hands and gave him a shivery confirmation. 'Oh I'm sure.'

'You already have the proof you wanted,' Bolan pointed out.

She gave her head an emphatic shake and whispered, 'Well not quite.'

Bolan showed her a solemn smile and said, 'Everybody turns off at the same switch, Ann. It's what turns us on that makes the difference.' He waved a hand over her head in a mock ceremonial gesture. 'I now pronounce you a natural woman.'

'Mack for God's sake make love to me,' she pleaded in a half-strangled little voice.

He whispered a very ragged, 'Okay,' and pushed himself clear and began coming away from his clothing.

She watched him through heavy-lidded eyes, lying still as death except for the rapid rise and fall of her breath, the pink tip of a delicate tongue curled into the corner of parted lips.

He snapped off the gunleather and dropped it to the floor, very close to the bed, attacked the skinsuit then halted suddenly, aware of her intent gaze.

She giggled and said, 'Carry on. I've seen it before. I put you to bed yesterday, remember?'

'You haven't seen it like this before,' he growled, and peeled off the suit and threw it at her.

She squealed and flipped over onto all fours, and Bolan scooped her up and dragged her off the bed. She clung to him and their lips merged again, after which he told her, 'I'll have a bath first, m'lady. Want to come in with me?'

She nodded starry-eyed approval of the suggestion and Bolan carried her down from the stage of a bed and deposited her at the edge of the bubbling-fountain pool. She slipped out of the bra and clung to Bolan's shoulder with one hand as she stepped out of the silken bikini.

Then she froze in that position, her fingers digging into Bolan's shoulder, and she let out a scream that shivered him clear to his feet. He overreacted, snatching her away from the pool with a violence that sent her sprawling across the floor. Then he saw what she had seen, and he was shivered all over again.

The dead eyes of Harry Parks were staring up at him from beneath the water. The naked body was arched back with the head drawn between the knees in almost the same position in which Edwin Charles had died, and he was bound into that position with a thick tapestry cord. A heavy metal figurine was holding the body submerged.

Bolan went into the water and pulled him out while Ann Franklin had a mild case of hysterics on the sidelines. Except for bruises made by the bindings, no marks of violence showed on the body. Harry Parks had undoubtedly died down there with his lungs full of water, his nose barely beneath the surface and straining to break clear – it all showed in those horribly staring dead eyes. Rigor mortis had arrived, and Bolan did not even attempt to straighten the body. He covered the crouching figure with an oval throw rug and led Ann Franklin back to the bed, rounded up her clothes, and tossed them to her.

'You'd better get dressed,' he said listlessly.

She did so mechanically. Bolan got into his and went directly to the bar. He found the brandy and poured two stiff doses and carried them to the bed. Ann took hers without looking at him, and held the glass with both hands, peering down into the liquid as though hoping to find something written there.

Bolan tossed his down, then whirled about and heaved the glass against the far wall. It hit with a crash, and Ann flinched.

Bolan muttered, 'Hell, I am *sick* of this!'

The girl woodenly murmured, 'Poor Harry,' and delicately tasted her brandy.

'Poor Harry's been dead a long time,' Bolan informed her. 'When was the last time you were up here?'

'Last night,' she whispered. 'For a moment.'

'What time last night?'

'Directly after you left here. Or a short time after. The police had a few questions. We answered them. Then I came up to change my clothes. I went straight back out. Harry and the Major were in the bar. I had a word of goodnight with them. Then I went straightaway to Queen's House. That was the last time I saw Harry.' Her eyes strayed to the lump at the bottom of the platform. She shivered and added, 'Alive.'

'So about what time was that?' Bolan persisted.

'I suppose ... shortly past twelve. I had thought that you would come to Queen's House. I waited until two o'clock. Then I went to the museum. The police were there and we had quite a fuss. You know about all that.'

Bolan said, 'Yeah.' He paced the platform for a moment, then told her, 'Okay, get your stuff, we're getting out of here.'

'It's dangerous for you out there,' she argued quietly. 'And we shouldn't be trying for Brighton until—'

'It's liable to get a hell of a lot more dangerous for both of us right here,' he told her. 'And to hell with Brighton. I've got things to do. Come on.'

He turned away and went quickly down to the main level. She scrambled after him, pausing for a moment beside the remains of Harry Parks to gaze frozenly at the tragic lump, then she snatched up her coat and hurried on through. Bolan was waiting for her at the door, and he was looking at the apartment as though he would never see it again and wanted to remember it.

Ann caught the look and joined him in it. 'Well,' she said with a soft sigh, 'I'm sure it's dreadfully callous of me to feel so selfishly at such a time, but ...' She sighed again. 'I suppose it simply shall never happen.'

He knew what she meant. He told her, 'This place is a fantasy, Ann.'

'Yes, quite,' she agreed. 'It's rather like pornography, isn't it?'

'You don't need it,' he said.

'You haven't proved that to me yet.'

He said, 'You proved it to yourself. Now come on, let's get out of here.'

'Poor Harry,' she murmured as they went out the door. 'What a revolting way to die.'

He led her down the stairway and replied, 'It's an even more revolting way to live.'

'Yes, I see what you mean.'

They moved on thru the lobby and Bolan said, 'Charles told me that all of this is a symbol of our times. I mean this Sadian bit. What do you suppose he meant by that, Ann?'

'I suppose he meant that we live in a pornographic age.'

He steered her through the lobby and onto Frith Street. 'No, I think he meant something more than that.'

They hurried around the corner and along the side street to Ann's vehicle. She had been thinking about Bolan's last statement. 'Well, I doubt that you'll ever know one way or another,' she told him.

'Don't be so sure about that,' he said. 'We just might be on our way to an answer right now.'

'Where are we going, Mack?'

'We're going to the Tower of London, m'lady.'

'Oh Mack! In broad daylight and with bobbies scouring the city for you? Whatever for?'

'Maybe,' he replied, 'for a glimpse at this symbol of our times.'

What Bolan did not realize then was that he had been walking in the shadow of that symbol since his arrival in England. It was a symbol of death.

CHAPTER SEVENTEEN

THE RAVENS

NOT one but two table-top conferences had been under-way at the Mafia's London headquarters at the moment of Bolan's telephone conversation with Leo Turrin. A meeting in the library was chaired by Joe Staccio, and was attended by Turrin and the crew leaders of the peace delegation.

Staccio had told them, 'Just in case any of you are wondering why I brought such a large bunch over, I just want you all to understand this one thing. It only takes one man to talk peace. That one man is me. Now Leo here is the contact man, and maybe he can get Bolan to stand still long enough to hear what I got to say. Okay, that takes care of the peace end. So you're asking yourselves, why'd Joe bring the rest of us along? Well, here's exactly why. Arnie Farmer is a *Capo*, and we all have to respect him for that. But he's also a double-dealing rat at times, and we have to respect him for that also. That's why you're here, the rest of you. Arnie Farmer I know is going to try crossing me up. I feel it in my bones. And he's liable to get me killed. I want you all to feel *that* in *your* bones.'

A Staccio underboss pushed a heavy ashtray into a slide down the mahogany table and growled, 'He better not try it, Joe.'

'Well, he's going to and we all know it. But listen, he will be the outlaw in this thing. I just want you all to understand that, and to know where you stand in this thing. When Arnie Farmer crosses me, he's also crossing the will of the *Commissione*, as decided in full council before I took on this responsibility. So you know where you stand. I brought you over here to keep Arnie Farmer honest. I guess I don't have to say any more than that.'

There followed a spirited discussion of strategy, defense, and of ways and means of convincing Mack Bolan that an honorable and rewarding peace could be his. Turrin was asked to recount various intimate details of his earlier association with Bolan, 'so as to give us all a better picture of how this boy thinks,' and Turrin did so, relating the episode at Pittsfield with as much honesty as he thought practicable.

Toward the end of this recitation, Bolan's call came through. Turrin carried on his end of the conversation under the eyes and ears of 'Staccio's Peace Corps', the tag laughingly applied to the delegation by its own members.

When he hung up, Turrin grinned at the New York boss and told him, 'Okay, my feelers are starting to pay off. This boy here knows Bolan from way back. I think this is what we been looking for.'

'Yeah, I got that,' Staccio replied, a worried frown furrowing his forehead. 'Now how many other ears you figure were listening on extensions around here?'

Still grinning, Turrin said, 'Probably at least half a dozen. That's why I picked this Tower of London for the meet. We can protect a meet like that, huh Joe?'

'You bet your ass we can,' Staccio growled. His eyes snapped to one of the crew leaders. 'You get out there, Bobby, and keep an eye on the ratpack. If anybody leaves, you report it back to me right quick.'

The crew leader hurried out, and the other leaders of the Peace Corps bent their heads to the strategic problems of the moment.

Meanwhile another conference under that same roof involved Arnie Farmer Castiglione and his legion of headhunters. A large drawing room was filled to standing-room capacity with crew leaders alone, and the atmosphere of the room was charged with the tension and excitement of the task being outlined there.

Castigilione, of course, was running the meeting.

Nick Trigger and Danno Giliamo flanked the big man at the table. Both wore the look of a slightly whipped dog.

The farmer was saying, 'Now these two boys here know that I'm giving it to you straight. This Bolan has made a couple of monkeys out of both of 'em. He's got them so rattled they can't even both tell the same story about what's been going on around here. You all know what this Bolan can do, you know what he's been doing to us right along. A couple of the old men back home think they can tame this wild man and make 'im one of us. But you go talk to Frank Buck about that. He'll tell you that no wild animal ever gets really tamed, it's liable to turn on you at any time.'

'Yeah, I tried to raise a baby alligator once,' put in a hood from Chicago. He stuck out a hand, revealing the loss of several fingers. 'Look what that son of a bitch done to me.'

'Shortfingers knows what I'm talking about,' Castiglione commented, glowering around the table. 'You don't make deals with wild men, and you don't invite them into your house and turn over the bedroom keys, and you especially don't give 'im a gun and tell 'im to run your palace guard for you.'

'Christ no!' agreed another man.

'Bet your ass it's Christ no, but that's exactly what these tired old men back home want to do – not all of 'em now, I'm not talking against no special families. I'm just saying a few put the pressure on, and what the hell could the rest of us say? Huh? We had to go along. But listen, only one or two are all for this thing, this peace bullshit. You notice, all of you boys notice that you've come from every part of the country, and you were sent to join my head party, and you all realize that. But now listen, how many of you boys would like to see this wildman Bolan carrying a *Commissione* badge, and steppin' into the shoes of the Talifero brothers?'

At that suggestion every ounce of blood drained from Nick Trigger's face, nor was Danno Giliamo looking over-joyed at the prospect. Their reactions were lost, however, in the general ruckus spreading throughout the room. Everybody was talking to everybody else, and the meeting fell into brief disarray, then a telephone in the corner sounded and the chatter quickly subsided as all eyes turned to the instrument.

Giliamo pushed back his chair and walked quietly to the telephone, though it had stopped ringing, and delicately lifted the receiver. He turned about to stare at Castiglione as he listened in on the Turrin-Bolan conversation, then he hung up and returned to the conference table.

'Okay, what was that all about?' Arnie Farmer growled.

'That,' Danno thoughtfully announced, 'was Leo the Pussy making his contact.'

'Awright, don't save yourself any secrets,' the Farmer demanded.

'Well, he's meeting this boy at some Tower of London at ten thirty. But listen. That boy sure sounded like Bolan's voice. I mean, not exactly, but Christ, it give me the creeps, I think that was Bolan right there on the phone.'

Castiglione glared at him while his mind ran through the implications presented. Nick Trigger, though, scowled at Danno and said, 'When've you ever heard Bolan's voice before?'

'I've heard a lot of things you've never dreamed about,' Danno snapped back. 'I think I'm right, I think it was Bolan himself.'

'You two shut up!' Arnie Farmer commanded. 'What time is it now?'

Someone replied, 'It's almost eight thirty, I guess I run my watch ahead right.'

'Yeah, it's eight thirty,' Nick Trigger growled.

'All right Nick, you get out there and get some boys on their toes. Danno, you go with 'im and make sure he don't get rattled or mixed up or something, both of you watch each other.' He dismissed them with a disgusted glance. 'Rest of you boys get your heads in and listen closely to what I'm going to tell you. Now don't get fucked up on this, I mean, you listen close 'cause I'm only gonna run through this once. Now listen . . .'

Nick Trigger and Danno Giliamo found themselves alone in the hall and glaring at each other. Nick muttered, 'That rotten old bastard. Where does he get off talking to me like that?'

Danno lit a cigarette with angrily shaking hands and said, 'You remember what we agreed to in the car last night, that Arnie the Farmer is a rotten bastard.'

'Yeah, that's *one* thing I remember.'

'Well, what're you going to do about that, Nick? I mean, this Bolan deal. You heard what the old bastard said. They're thinking of turning over your job to Bolan, I mean the job that's yours by rights. And even if Arnie gets to Bolan first, you know he's not going to see you up there on the hard arm, you know that. It only takes one guy like that to squeeze you out forever, Nick. And that job is yours, by rights.'

'By right, yeah,' Nick Trigger muttered.

'Well, I guess we know where we stand.'

'I guess we do. Listen, Danno, I guess we are in the same boat. Now I don't know what happened last night and I don't give a damn. We're in the same boat and I guess we better start doing some bailing.'

'I'd like to show Arnie Farmer what a monkey feels like,' Danno said. 'You just can't let him get to Bolan first, Nick.'

'Don't you worry, he won't. And neither will Leo the Pussy.'

'You got something in mind, Nick?'

'You could say that, Danno. Yeah, you could say that.' Nick Trigger, as a matter of fact, had quite a lot in his mind.

Bolan and Ann reached the Tower Hill district a full hour in advance of the appointment with Leo Turrin, and Bolan prowled the streets of the area relentlessly for most of thirty minutes, getting the feel of the land. Then he parked at a tour bus station and told the girl, 'They'll let me get in there, all right. The problem will be in getting out with my head still on.'

'But you can't go walking about in there,' she protested. 'Someone will recognize you, and then we shall see a C.I.D. convention at London Tower.'

He smiled and told her, 'Most people aren't all that observant. How often have you walked past a friend on the street without noticing him? Those people in there will be looking at crown jewels and British history, and they'll all be wishing they had four eyes to take it all in. They won't be looking at me.'

'The staff will,' she assured him.

'To them I'll just be another bloody tourist,' he replied, grinning. 'Look, stop worrying. This is my kind of warfare.'

She was scruffling around in the glove compartment. 'At the very least you can wear these,' she urged, handing over tinted lenses in weird wire frames. 'They're adjustable, so no excuses.'

He chuckled and slid the earpieces out and bent them onto his temples, then stared at her owlishly through the tinted lenses. 'How's this?'

She cried, 'Oh Mack!' and threw herself into his arms.

They lingered in a kiss, then he gently disentangled himself and told her, 'Stay loose now. Get this car moving and keep circling. Try to make it past here at least once every five minutes. But at the first sound of gunfire, you skedaddle and damn quick. Don't worry about me, I'll find a way through. If we get split up, meet me at the museum. I doubt that anyone will be expecting me to show up there again.'

She nodded and slid her arms back around his neck. 'Don't you dare get yourself killed,' she whispered. 'I doubt that I could survive it.'

He chuckled, kissed her again, and left her sitting there with saucer eyes. He glanced back, saw that she was crying, and threw her a reassuring wave, then mingled in with a tour party which was just then debusing.

It cost him four shillings admission to the grounds, and he paid another two shillings for access to the interior areas. He had almost a half hour to kill, and he used this time for a casual look around at the fabulous complex, once the castle of William the Conqueror. He saw the room where the Little Princes were smothered and visited the Armories in the White Tower for a glimpse of King Henry VIII's armor. Then he went back onto the grounds where he engaged in a friendly conversation with a colorfully costumed *Beefeater* – the name given the Tower guards. The guy showed him the clipped-wing ravens, and told him that they were the symbol of the Tower.

Bolan thought, yeah, those ravens were a symbol of the time, too – like old Charles' Sadian symbol. Civilized men had that same frustration constantly with them, that same clipped-wing freedom of the ravens. Throw away everything that makes you a man, man, and then *be a man.*

Nuts, Bolan thought. He hadn't been able to settle for the clipped-wing type of existence urged upon him by the Pittsfield cops; he'd decided to be an eagle . . . and now here he was practically a dead duck, despite his brave reassurances to Ann Franklin.

The time was ten twenty. He wandered back and found the scaffolding where crowned heads had rolled, the final stop for kings and queens who'd found the power of reigning a bit too heady. Men never learned anything, Bolan was thinking. The scramble for power and the lusting for wealth would never end, it would go on and on as long as ravens had clipped wings.

He was in a hell of a mood and he knew it. The Tower had done it to him, it had done something that all the macabre atmosphere of *Museum de Sade* had failed to do, and Bolan was beginning to get a glimmer of what old Edwin Charles had meant. The whole God damned world was bathed in blood, it had soaked into the earth behind every footprint of mankind, and the screams and groans of the tortured and the revolted and the shit-upon still lived on in every movement of the wind.

Yeah, dammit, that was what Charles had meant. The agony of mankind was only mirrored in the offbeat flesh routes that some men pursued. The reality of that agony would not be found in some pathetic devil's pantings over sado-masochistic pornography. The reality was buried in the core of that worldwide panting for power over other men's lives and the ruthless acquisition of wealth for the few at the expense of the many.

Thank you, Edwin Charles, Bolan said to a memory. You've reminded me what I'm all about.

And then it was 10:25 and Leo Turrin was making a quick approach with a very worried face.

Bolan muttered to himself, 'And here we go again. Another jug of blood for the ravens.'

CHAPTER EIGHTEEN

SHOWDOWN AT DE SADE

BOLAN shoved the glasses up onto his forehead and told Leo Turrin, 'I hope this turns out to be worth the risk.'

'I don't know about that,' the little *Mafioso* replied glumly. 'This has turned into an Olympic Game called *get Bolan*, and it's anybody's game at the moment.'

Bolan said, 'That means you brought a convoy.'

'*Did* I. It would be funny if it wasn't so damned serious. You may have a hard time believing this, Sarge, but right now you've got four big mean Mafia crews protecting your hide.'

'You brought them with you?' Bolan asked, his eyebrows rising into unhappy peaks.

'No other way. Arnie's head part is swarming all over. I smell a shootout, brother against brother, and all because of your hide, buddy.'

Bolan chuckled. His tensions were leaving him. He said, 'Okay, let's make it quick, then. I wouldn't want to miss the party.'

Turrin took him by the arm and walked him along the scaffolding of Execution Row. 'Okay, first the poop Edwin Charles. Brognola hit a blank there right away. Charles' army folder has a classified seal on it, and the British won't even talk about him. Via our own army intelligence, though, Hal learned that this guy was retired with honors 15 years ago, with the rank of Brigadier.'

Bolan's eyes sparkled and he said, 'Bingo.'

'Well, maybe it means something to you. Not to me. Here's the interesting part. Charles went back on the active list briefly in 1960, at the age of sixty-three. How about that? He served for eight months, then retired again. Our

145

intelligence on him ends as of four months ago when this same old man was re-activated again, assignment undisclosed – buried somewhere beneath that security seal.'

Bolan whistled softly under his breath. 'What was he doing during that eight months of 1960?'

'Brognola doesn't know, but it may not be any coincidence that the British cracked an espionage ring at about that time.'

'That's getting a bit far out,' Bolan commented. 'I mean, espionage . . .'

'No connection necessary,' Turrin assured him. 'But you tell me something. What was this Edwin Charles doing just before he died?'

'Doing? He was supposedly working as an electronics mechanic and security watchman in a house of kinks.'

'Well, there's your tie. Electronics. It's Charles' speciality. He was in on the ground floor in the art of electronic spying for the British.'

'Okay, I have to think about that. What else did you get?'

'This Major Stone. No secrets there. Cashiered out of the British regulars in 1956 for cruelty to his troops, repeated incidents. Also some grisly charges from various civilians in the Mideast. He's not retired, just fired, so he's carrying that title around in his hip pocket. Brognola has a thick file on him, gathered from here and there. The guy has gone from an obscure army major, noted only for his discharge in disgrace, to a very wealthy man with little visible means of support.'

Bolan's face was screwed into a thoughtful grimace. 'Okay, anything else?'

'That's all of any value on Charles and Stone. But here comes the bonus, if you can figure a way to use it . . . I can't. This intel came in at the last minute and I haven't even had time to think about it myself. Nick Trigger came to England under the alias of Nicholas Woods. He's always been a rodman, never a speculator. Consequently, he never accumulated much money – spent it as fast as he got it. Now keep that picture. Okay, now enter Nicholas Woods upon the British scene. All of a sudden the guy has two secret bank accounts in Geneva and there's enough between those accounts to keep him like a sultan for the rest of a long lifetime.'

Bolan asked, 'What does "all of a sudden" mean?'

'It means within the past few months.'

'Okay, I agree it's interesting. But not exactly earth-shattering.'

Turrin shrugged. 'Except that jolly old Nick is knocking down on the family. He's obviously got some hot action of his own going over here, and that's a very definite no-no. And there's more to it than that. He's also got money going openly back and forth in a partnership with a legitimate business enterprise here in London, and there's some sort of a connection between this and the Swiss bank accounts.'

'What's this legit thing he has?'

'A night club called Soho Psych.'

Bolan's feet hit the floor and stayed there. Turrin halted and turned back to give him a puzzled stare. 'What's wrong?'

Bolan muttered, 'You just popped me square in the guts.'

'This night club means something to you? I haven't been in town long enough to—'

'I'm afraid it means a hell of a lot, Leo. Did Brognola tell you who Nick's partner is?'

Turrin shook his head. 'I don't believe he'd had time to dig that far. Anyway, what I wanted to tell you . . . Hal is thrilled to death over this peace offering. He says quote tell him for God's sake to take it unquote. He thinks it's the greatest thing since Joe Valacchi's Atlanta concert.'

All the fire seemed to have drained out of Bolan. He muttered, 'You know I can't, Leo. I can't even let those people *think* they've won. I've got to keep them falling over each other's asses for just as long as I can keep it all together.'

'You haven't heard what Staccio is empowered to offer you, Sarge. They want you to take over as lord high enforcer, or something along that line.'

Bolan smiled thinly. 'If you can't beat 'em, buy 'em or join 'em. That's their philosophy, Leo, and it always worked for them in the past. I won't let it work this time.' He was thinking of a twenty-six year old virgin beauty who must have wanted to beat the whole world, then simply decided to join it. 'No, I can't do it. I'll stay in my own jungle, thanks.'

'At least think it over,' Turrin urged. 'Brognola says he can damn sure work up an amnesty case for you once you get inside that *Commissione.*'

Bolan shook his head doggedly. 'No. Leave me alone, Leo. I have to do it my way.'

The Italian scowled unhappily, but replied, 'Okay, I respect your decision, even if I don't like it. So maybe you can use this dirt on Nick Trigger. Maybe you can drive a wedge in somewhere, turn things over good. I can't use it. It would be too far out of the character I've been building up these past five years.' He sighed. 'Anyway, that's all I've got. Now I suggest we split, and quick, before Arnie decides to come in looking.'

'Let's not leave you out in the cold,' Bolan said quietly. 'Tell your Ambassador of Peace that I refuse to consider the idea until I get back home. Tell him we'll get together over there and talk about this thing.'

Turrin smiled sourly and said, 'Yeah, that'll save me some face.'

'You go on out,' Bolan suggested. 'I'll leave my own way.'

They shook hands and Turrin said, 'I saw a good place to go over the fence.'

Bolan grinned, showing an echo of his earlier fire. 'I saw it too. Thanks, Leo. Take care.'

Turrin said, 'You too,' and spun off in a rapid departure. He looked back and waved from the corner, then disappeared.

Bolan took his own prearranged way out, back past the *Beefeaters* and the clipped-wing ravens and to the soft spot in the wall he'd staked out during his recon.

From down in front somewhere came the sudden crackling of weapons, just as Bolan found his toehold and boosted himself toward the top.

Then hell was swirling out there, with the booming chops of heavy Thompsons mingling with the lighter rattling of small automatics, and Bolan knew that the enemy had engaged itself.

Leo was right; it was almost funny.

Bolan swung his leg over to sprawl across the top of the wall, and found another almost-funny event awaiting him. Immediately below him a semi-circle of armed gunners were standing around the open door, of a shiny limousine and a fat man with curly white hair was stepping into their midst.

Bolan had no trouble whatever recognizing Arnie Farmer Catiglione; he was lying almost on top of him. The Beretta sprung into Bolan's fist and he called down, 'Arnie!'

The white head snapped around and Arnie Farmer saw death contemplating him. He froze there in slack-jawed dismay as his human shield dissolved about him to the Parabellum rhythms of a softly coughing Beretta, and then it was just he and Bolan.

Arnie was grunting, 'Kill 'im, kill 'im!' and reaching for a revolver that had dropped from a dead man's hand when he heard Bolan's cold tones clearly enunciating, 'I pronounce you dead, Arnie,' and the miserable bastard was sitting there on the roof of Arnie's own car and a small flame was whistling out of the muzzle of the Beretta and something fearsome was plunging in between Arnie's eyes and doing horrible things to his head, and that was the final thing that Arnie Farmer knew.

It had been but a brief and relatively quiet delay for Bolan. He ran down the street, away from the sounds of warfare, and as he approached the first intersection he spotted the little rental sedan that meant Ann Franklin was still on station.

Bolan debated with his emotions momentarily, then he set his jaw and ran on to meet her. She had the door open for him and he slid in with the car still moving. He snapped her a quick look and saw that same scared look she'd worn that first time he'd jumped into a moving vehicle with her at the wheel.

She said not a word, nor did he, and he was fighting the high-G takeoff and trying to feed a fresh clip into the Beretta when he became aware of the unmistakable presence of a gun at his neck.

Bolan swore and damned and raged at himself for losing that emotional debate, but his voice was calm as he said, 'Well, Major, I guess we finally get that talk.'

A dry chuckle sounded behind him and the voice of Major Stone confirmed his guess and posed the question at the same time. 'How were you so sure it was *me* behind you, Mr. Bolan?'

'It just began to fall into place a short while ago,' Bolan told him. His eyes flicked to the girl and he added, 'It *all* fell in.'

She cried, 'Mack . . .' in a smothery little voice, and Major Stone commanded, 'Remain quiet please, Ann!'

Bolan quietly said, 'All the crying concern for the security of your members. You've been gouging them all along, for one hell of a long time before Nick Trigger came on the scene. So why did you import *me*, Major? Was Nick muscling in on your gravy train?'

'Shut up, Bolan,' the Major said. 'Pass your pistol back here, carefully now.'

Bolan did both, and sat in silent contemplation of his errors as Ann expertly wheeled through the streets of midday London. Twice they were delayed at intersections, once by a screaming procession of police vehicles descending on Tower Hill, and both times Bolan briefly considered making a break but capitulated to logic and to the ancient hope that has forever dwelt in the breasts of nearly-dead men – he would not rush death, he would wait it out and see what developed.

Nothing whatever developed throughout that silent ride, and when Ann parked the car at the curb outside *Museum de Sade* Bolan began to get the idea that the most likely thing to develop for him now was mortal agony. His skin was crawling with the memory of those torture cells as he quit the car and went up the steps ahead of Major Stone. He paused at the door and stared back down at the car; Ann was remaining there, obviously.

He called back, 'Okay, the pact is dissolved. You may as well come in and watch the grand finale.'

There was no movement from the vehicle. The stiff little man jabbed Bolan's ribs with hard steel and pushed him on inside. Nick Trigger was at the bar in the clubroom, drinking gin straight out of a bottle. He came slightly unglued at the sight of Bolan, and then crowed with delight upon noticing the pistol in the Major's hand. He ran over and slugged Bolan with the back of his hand and yelled, 'You rotten shit!'

Bolan shook off the blow and muttered, 'It takes one to know one.'

The Major shoved Nick away. 'None of that just now!' he snapped. 'Keep your distance! You're aware of the danger of this man!'

'Sure, just be patient, Nick,' Bolan said. 'You'll get your chance to watch me squirm.'

'*Scream* is the word, Bolan,' the Major corrected him. He shoved Bolan on across the clubroom and marched him through the travesty of erotic delights and up to the maze. Bolan had not until that moment caught the significance of the labial doorway. *Back into the womb*, it meant. Not merely death, but an unborning.

Bolan halted in the gray light of the little ante-room and snarled, 'You're not going to lock me into one of those things while I'm living, Major.'

Stone replied. 'You are quite wrong about that, Bolan.'

Bolan saw the barrel of the pistol chopping toward him. He managed to get inside and take it on the shoulder and he abruptly lost all strength in that arm, but he was plowing forward in a body-block that would have made his old football coach proud, and the three men hit the floor in a sprawling tangle.

Nick Trigger was trying to smother him with his big belly and Bolan was fighting to get clear and become the first man up. He threw Nick away from him and went into a roll, then the barrel of the Major's revolver again loomed into view and smashed into his skull with a jarring crunch.

Bolan grunted and pitched onto his back, not at all the way out but sick and groggy and utterly without strength. He was aware of being pushed, and dragged in a background of foul mouthings by Nick Trigger and the hoarse panting of Major Stone. Then his clothes were being dragged away from him and the disembodied voice of Nick Trigger was saying, 'Aw shit, why go through all this?'

But apparently the Major felt some compulsion to mix pleasure with business, and even in his giddy state Bolan recognized and was appalled by the depths of the man's sickness.

Stone was telling Nick, 'Do not presume to deny me my simple pleasures, my friend. After all, it is you who demanded immediate action. I would have given the poor fellow another day or two, if only for Ann's sake.'

Through Bolan's swirling nausea, Nick was arguing, 'Christ, this is no time for pleasures, yours or hers or anybody else's. I mean, we got the two finks outta the picture and I'm in a hell of a bind over on my side now. I gotta have this guy's head; to hell with your kicks.'

The Major was breathing heavily and clamping something cold and hard about Bolan's forehead. He tried to struggle away, but a knee in his throat held him pinned and he was simply too weak to do anything about it. Stone's stiffly precise voice was saying, 'There wouldn't have been the problem of the two *finks*, as you put it, but for your monumental greed, Nick. In all the years I've been at this, I've incurred not one serious threat, not one. And now six months after your intrusion into my little world, I find myself the object of scrutiny from every direction. No. No, Nick. Don't attempt to hurry me along now.'

Clamps were going about Bolan's ankles. The hands down there were fumbling about, as though trembling almost out of control. Bolan fought the nausea and willed his strength to return. It would not.

'Shit, you're just plain crazy!' Nick yelled.

'Get out of here!' Stone cried. 'Will you get out of here?'

'You kiss my ass!' Nick retorted. 'You fuckin' queer, you're gonna fuck up everything.'

'Look who is speaking!' The Major's voice came with cutting sarcasm. '*You* are the one who said bring Bolan over! *You* are the one who said let *Bolan* take the blame! *You* are the one who said—'

'Awright, now I'm saying let's kill 'im and get it over with. This kind of shit gives me the creeps and you know it.

152

Anyway, I'm the one under the pressure, not you. I'm the one crossed up the family, not you. If you'd just listened when I wanted to drop those finks in the river with cement suits on, there wouldn't be—'

'Oh to be sure, that would have been jolly. Brigadier Edwin Charles turns up in the Thames from his latest assignment and where does that leave the ambitious Mr. Nicholas Woods? Not, of course, to mention the Sade Society and our beautiful little goldmine. Honestly, Nick, sometimes you behave as a very dull fellow. Now here, give me a hand with this beauty, will you?'

Bolan was being hauled and lifted, the clamps at head and ankles beginning to take the weight and compress the flesh over protesting bones. Then he was up and momentarily floating free only to be abruptly jerked to a spine-crunching arrest. Full consciousness returned on floodwaves of shriekingly alarmed nerve-centers, and Bolan knew with a tortured clarity where he was and what sort of a pickle he was in.

His hands were manacled behind his back and he was suspended from the ceiling by three chains. One of these was attached to a steel band that was fitted about his forehead, the other two held his ankles, and he was dangling in a belly-down suspension several feet above the floor.

Nick stood in a corner, glowering at the Major, Stone was shoving a boxlike affair across the cell, obviously intent on positioning it beneath Bolan's belly. It slid under easily, clearing by several inches, then the Major appeared at Bolan's head. He looked into his eyes and said, 'Ah good, our astronaut is conscious. Listen and let me explain our little game. I've put a clever machine beneath you, Bolan. It's a simple little box with a spring-loaded mechanism inside and a rather wicked steel blade mounted on the outside, across the top. When I release the brake, the blade will move quickly back and forth across the top of the box, you see. Now it might scrape you a bit here and there if you get too relaxed. Keep your spine nice and straight, though, and you'll have nothing to fear. And be on the lookout for, uh, dangling objects. You might lose something you prize highly. Be ready, now, keep a stiff back there, that's a good fellow.'

Something went *spronnng* beneath him, and he felt the air of the whisking blade as it moved back and forth just below.

Bolan had known for quite some time that he was not going to live forever. He had known that intimate association with death on many occasions, and he had long been prepared to die. But not like this. Not a slow and gradual scraping away. First it would be genitals, probably in one or two whacks, as soon as the muscles around the spine atrophied and collapsed and sent him plunging into range of that shuttling blade. Then the weakness and further collapse would sag the abdomen down there, and layer by layer of him would be laid open until he was totally disembowelled and hacked in two.

Well, he would not take it that way. He himself had always tried to kill quick and painlessly, and he was going to go out the same way. He steeled himself and began preparing the command to his muscular structure that would send him all the way down in one disemboweling plunge.

And then he became aware of a movement at the doorway dead ahead of him. Ann Franklin stepped in, and she had the big Weatherby cradled tightly to her body, and he thought thank God she's going to give it to me right.

The big piece roared and Bolan saw Major Stone flopping along the desk with his pants down about his ankles; another thunderous report and Nick Trigger was lending parts of himself to the walls of the corner.

The Weatherby was clattering to the floor and Ann was beneath him, supporting his weight with her own back and kicking frantically at the box.

Yeah, so it had happened, and he was entirely in her hands after all.

He mumbled, 'Thanks, Ann, and all that,' and then he passed out.

EPILOGUE

It has been a curious and a furious 40 hours in England. Bolan had launched an assault upon Soho, and Soho had assaulted him back. A symbol of the times, Edwin Charles had told him; and certainly that symbol covered a great deal more than 'this crackling museum of ours'. The domain of violence lurked deeply in every place where men flung themselves off into a shallow forgetfulness of the greater meanings of life, and it surfaced wherever greed and the lust for power were present.

Some good men had died during those brief hours, but so had a pile of rotten ones. Bolan had to figure that as a plus on the world's balance sheet.

An entire vault of damning pornographic films had been uncovered in the home of the late Mervyn Stone, and burned, and enshrined in a little urn in the entrance hall of the *Museum de Sade*. Bolan saw that as a conditional plus for the future of a great nation, and as a very graphic hint to the men whose images had been on that film.

Open warfare had erupted between dissident elements of the most corruptive criminal empire in history, and Leo Turrin read that as a very strong plus.

The mystery had unravelled to Bolan's satisfaction, and while this had no place as a plus or a minus, it did give him relative peace of mind. Major Stone had obviously been bleeding his 'members' for a number of years, but not in a manner to cause undue excitement. When the Mafia began muscling in, however, the repercussions were felt in the higher echelons of government, and a quietly delicate investigation was launched. Complicating this circumstance was the item of Nick Trigger's greed; he lost his power over Mervyn Stone by entering into a clandestine financial arrangement with him, in direct violation of the powers that ruled his life. Both of these men panicked when a harmless old tinkerer was revealed to them as an agent of Her Majesty's Government, and this was where Bolan came in. Nick Trigger had walked a tightrope between his obligations to family and obligations to self, and that rope had begun to fray long before the final break.

All in all, Bolan had to score the battle as a definite plus for the upward movements of mankind, and as a shattering loss to the other side of the coin.

As regarding Ann Franklin, he did not know just exactly how to mark the scorecard. He tried to impart the idea of saving grace to his hostess in the Franklin bathroom at Queen's House as he groomed himself and repaired minor damages to his person. He sprinkled an antiseptic solution on his lacerated scalp while he told her, 'You can't blame yourself for anything that happened. That is, unless you want to feel responsible for the fact that I'm still alive. You're to blame for that, all right.'

She was giving him that winsome look from the doorway. 'You're too kind,' she replied.

'Look, you just got conned. It happens to the best of us.'

'Well, I wouldn't have called him, you know, except that I was so stupidly positive that you were wrong about him. And I was frightened silly. I've been going to the Major with my problems for as long as I can remember.' She raised her shoulders and dropped them in a dainty slump. 'I thought he could help us,' she added in a tiny voice.

Bolan was grinning. He told her, 'Sometimes it's hard to separate friends from enemies. Like Danno Giliamo. My contact tells me that old Danno is really on the carpet over this deal. He thought he was conning Nick, and all the time he was getting it right in the back. Those screwballs had formed a third front. They were going to deliver my head to the *Commissione* in a paper bag. Imagine that?'

Ann shuddered. 'No worse than me, I'm sure. And that's doubly true if they were actually running money through my club accounts, as you've intimated.'

Her face was screwed into an agonizing fit of indecision. Bolan chuckled and said, 'Okay, what is it?'

She said, 'Whether you want to hear it or not, Mack, I simply must get this out of my system. Honestly, I still wasn't certain as to just exactly what the Major had in mind until I walked in there and saw it. It's that military mastery of his, I suppose. He always did have me thoroughly cowed. And when he joined me outside the Tower, he told me that I mustn't worry about you, that he would save you if he had to put a gun to your head. Silly me, I believed him. It was that last thing you shouted at me from the stoop that turned my mind to thinking, I mean to *really* thinking.'

'I told you all bets were off.'

'No, you said that our pact was dissolved. And now. Let's get this out of my system also. *Is* it dissolved, Mack?'

He gave her a solemn inspection and said, 'Don't you think that's best?'

She shook her head. 'No. I remain in your hands, if you'll have it that way.'

Almost painfully he said, 'Plus.'

'What?'

He showed her a long, tender smile and told her, 'You're a plus. Keep it that way for the right time, the right place, the right guy.'

'You are the right guy,' she murmured.

'Wrong time and place, m'lady,' he said regretfully, and walked past her and into the bedroom. He snugged into his gunleather and put on his jacket, then went over and cracked the blinds for a window recon.

'You're leaving now, aren't you?' Ann whispered.

He nodded his head, rather sadly she thought. 'Yeah. That time has come again.'

'Where will you go?'

'Home ... wherever that is.'

'And how will you get there?'

He smiled and said, 'Through the jungle, m'lady. That's the only way.' He picked up his gear and strode to the front door. When he looked back she was standing just inside the bedroom and following him with a wistful smile.

He waved to her and she waved back. 'Thanks, and all that,' she called softly.

He grinned and went out. Somewhere out there in those wet wild woods was a trail home. He might find it, and he might not. But he had to try.

157

One thing he knew he would find:

Through the Jungle very softly flits a shadow
and a sigh. He is *Fear*, O Little hunter, he is *Fear*!

The little hunter struck out across the shadows and was enveloped in them, and became a part of them, and knew that he would live there ... and that one day he would die there.

The Executioner was blitzing on.

A SELECTION OF FINE READING
AVAILABLE IN CORGI BOOKS

General

☐ 552 09100 6   **FANNY HILL'S COOKBOOK**   *L. H. Braun & W. Adams* 40p
☐ 552 09169 3   **THE FASCINATING FORTIES**   *Barbara Cartland* 30p
☐ 552 09185 5   **THE FUNDAMENTALS OF SEX** (illustrated)
     Dr. Philip Cauthery & Dr. Martin Cole 50p
☐ 552 08926 5   **S IS FOR SEX**   *Robert Chartham* 50p
☐ 552 09151 0   **THE DRAGON AND THE PHOENIX**   *Eric Chou* 50p
☐ 552 98958 4   **THE ISLAND RACE Vol. 1**   *Winston S. Churchill* 125p
☐ 552 98959 5   **THE ISLAND RACE Vol. 2**   *Winston S. Churchill* 125p
☐ 552 08800 5   **CHARIOTS OF THE GODS?** (illustrated)   *Erich von Daniken* 35p
☐ 552 09073 2   **RETURN OF THE STARS** (illustrated)   *Erich von Daniken* 40p
☐ 552 09135 9   **THE HUMAN ANIMAL** (illustrated)   *Hans Hass* 40p
☐ 552 07400 4   **MY LIFE AND LOVES**   *Frank Harris* 65p
☐ 552 98748 4   **MAKING LOVE** (Photographs)   *Walter Hartford* 85p
☐ 552 08992 3   **MASTERING WITCHCRAFT**   *Paul Huson* 35p
☐ 552 09062 X   **THE SENSUOUS MAN**   'M' 35p
☐ 552 08069 1   **THE OTHER VICTORIANS**   *Steven Marcus* 50p
☐ 552 08010 1   **THE NAKED APE**   *Desmond Morris* 30p
☐ 552 09116 2   **A BRITISH SURVEY IN FEMALE SEXUALITY**
     Sandra McDermott 40p
☐ 552 09016 6   **GOLF TACTICS**   *Arnold Palmer* 45p
☐ 552 09044 1   **SEX ENERGY**   *Robert S. de Ropp* 35p
☐ 552 08880 3   **THE THIRTEENTH CANDLE**   *T. Lobsang Rampa* 35p
☐ 552 09145 6   **THE NYMPHO AND OTHER MANIACS**   *Irving Wallace* 40p

Western

☐ 552 09147 2   **IN THE DAYS OF VICTORIO** (illustrated)   *Eve Ball* 40p
☐ 552 09095 6   **APACHE**   *Will Levington Comfort* 30p
☐ 552 09170 7   **SUDDEN—DEAD OR ALIVE**   *Frederick H. Christian* 30p
☐ 552 09113 8   **TWO MILES TO THE BORDER No. 70**   *J. T. Edson* 25p
☐ 552 08288 0   **GOODNIGHT'S DREAM No. 50**   *J. T. Edson* 25p
☐ 552 08278 3   **FROM HIDE AND HORN No. 51**   *J. T. Edson* 25p
☐ 552 09112 X   **THE DAYBREAKERS**   *Louis L'Amour* 25p
☐ 552 09191 X   **TREASURE MOUNTAIN**   *Louis L'Amour* 30p
☐ 552 09165 0   **THE GALLOWS EXPRESS No. 19**   *Louis Masterson* 25p
☐ 552 09098 0   **PAINTED PONIES**   *Alan Le May* 35p
☐ 552 09097 2   **VALLEY OF THE SHADOW**   *Charles Marquis Warren* 35p

Crime

☐ 552 09164 2   **THERE GOES DEATH**   *John Creasey* 30p
☐ 552 09189 8   **FOUNDER MEMBER**   *John Gardner* 30p
☐ 552 08640 1   **RED FILE FOR CALLAN**   *James Mitchell* 30p
☐ 552 09073 5   **INNOCENT BYSTANDERS**   *James Munro* 30p
☐ 552 09181 2   **THE WALTER SYNDROME**   *Richard Neely* 35p
☐ 552 09111 1   **THE ERECTION SET**   *Mickey Spillane* 40p
☐ 552 09056 5   **SHAFT**   *Ernest Tidyman* 30p
☐ 552 09072 7   **SHAFT'S BIG SCORE**   *Ernest Tidyman* 30p

All these books are available at your bookshop or newsagent or can be ordered direct from the publisher. Just tick the titles you want and fill in the form below.

CORGI BOOKS, Cash Sales Department, P.O. Box 11, Falmouth, Cornwall.
Please send cheque or postal order. No currency, and allow 6p per book to cover the cost of postage and packing in the U.K. and overseas.

NAME ....

ADDRESS ....

(April 73) ....